Praise for *Bleakboy and H*

'A gentle book about how small acts of mercy, compassion and empathy can make a difference.' *Big Issue*

'Steven Herrick has nailed it again.' *Reading Time*

'This is a heartfelt story about friendship and family, doing the right thing and being yourself.' *Books+Publishing*

'Engaging and warm-hearted.' *Magpies*

'The upbeat message of empowerment through collective action strikes the right note.' *Canberra Times*

'This is a lovely book with wonderful engaging characters. By the end you are just hoping for the best for all of them – even Hunter!' *The Big Book Club*

'Herrick knows his audience.' *Saturday Age*

Steven Herrick was born in Brisbane, the youngest of seven children. At school his favourite subject was soccer, and he dreamed of football glory while he worked at various jobs. For the past thirty years he's been a full-time writer and regularly performs his work in schools throughout the world. Steven lives in the Blue Mountains with his partner Cathie, a belly dance teacher. They have two adult sons, Jack and Joe.

www.stevenherrick.com.au

Also by Steven Herrick

Young Adult

A place like this
Black painted fingernails
By the river
Cold skin
Lonesome howl
Love, ghosts and nose hair
Slice
The simple gift
Water bombs

Children

Do-wrong Ron
Love poems and leg-spinners
My life, my love, my lasagne
Naked bunyip dancing
Poetry to the rescue
Pookie Aleera is not my boyfriend
Rhyming boy
The place where the planes take off
Tom Jones saves the world
Untangling spaghetti

First published 2014 by University of Queensland Press
PO Box 6042, St Lucia, Queensland 4067 Australia
Reprinted 2014, 2015 (twice)

www.uqp.com.au
uqp@uqp.uq.edu.au

Cover design and illustration by Jo Hunt
Typeset in 12/16.5 pt Stempel Garamond by Post Pre-press Group, Brisbane
Printed in Australia by McPherson's Printing Group

Cataloguing-in-Publication Data
National Library of Australia
http://catalogue.nla.gov.au

Herrick, Steven, 1958- author.
Bleakboy and Hunter stand out in the rain / Steven Herrick.

ISBN 978 0 7022 5016 3 (pbk)
ISBN 978 0 7022 5266 2 (pdf)
ISBN 978 0 7022 5267 9 (epub)
ISBN 978 0 7022 5268 6 (kindle)

For primary school age.

Bullies–Fiction.
Schools–Fiction.

A823.3

University of Queensland Press uses papers that are natural, renewable
and recyclable products made from wood grown in sustainable forests.
The logging and manufacturing processes conform to the environmental
regulations of the country of origin.

UQP is not responsible for the content found on non-UQP websites.

BLEAKBOY and HUNTER

STAND OUT in the RAIN

Steven Herrick

UQP

1
Jesse

I look out the window. It's raining. Again. I press my face against the glass and breathe. The window fogs in the shape of a continent with more penguins than humans.

'Antarctica,' I whisper.

With my index finger, I draw an emperor penguin on the glass and step back to admire my artwork.

'That's a fairy penguin, not an emperor,' I murmur.

In the wardrobe, my choices for school are:

- Black t-shirt and blue shorts?
- Black pants and the shirt with the warrior queen fighting the dragon?
- Jeans?
- Overalls? What was mum thinking!

I select black pants and a plain black t-shirt. I hope it fits with my school uniform policy, which is, 'Wear whatever you like as long as it doesn't have negative images or advertising slogans'.

Is black negative? I put on white Dunlop Volleys, just in case.

Hanging on the wall above my bed is a poster of a long-haired bearded man standing in front of a religious cross. An orange-coloured aura radiates behind his head. In the foreground, a flock of worshippers kneel.

My parents don't like me having a religious idol on my wall. They tell me we're atheist, which sounds like someone with a sneezing disease. Dad says it means we don't worship false gods.

So, to make Mum and Dad happy, I call the dude on my wall, Trevor. At my old school, every Friday morning was devoted to learning about Trevor and his buddies. I went to the religious instruction class even though my parents gave me a letter saying I didn't have to go. I left the letter in the bottom of my backpack.

Trevor is my friend. I tell him my problems, of which there are many, and he listens and does something much better than my parents. He doesn't offer an opinion. He stands with his arms wide open, palms out, as if he's saying, 'Whatever you choose is fine'.

My name is Jesse James Jones. Call me Jesse. Don't call me triple j. I'm not a radio station, I'm an eleven-year-old boy.

Trevor looks down on me with understanding eyes. It's pretty tough going through life with a name that people make fun of. 'Even though I walk through the valley of the shadow—'

'Mum! Jesse's talking to himself again!' yells my sister Beth, from the next room.

'Jesse.' Mum's voice from the kitchen is reproachful, as though I've been caught doing something sinful.

Trevor's eyes plead with me to turn the other cheek.

'Easy for you to do, Trev. You've had lots of practice. Over two thousand years of understanding and tolerance.'

'Mum! Jesse has an imaginary friend!' Beth calls.

'And you never had a sister as annoying as mine. You were an only child,' I add.

Trevor looks as if he understands. I feel a presence in my room.

'Jesse,' the voice is soft and caring.

'Hi, Mum.'

She stands in the doorway wearing a flowing linen dress with lots of beads around her neck and stacks of bracelets on her wrists and ankles. Her dark hair is tied back in a ponytail. In her hand, she holds a slice of watermelon.

'Jesse,' she says again.

'Mum.'

'Jesse.'

Trevor stares.

'Jesse, you don't need an imaginary friend,' she glances toward Trevor. 'You've got us.'

Beth calls, 'Mum, have you stolen my yoga pants?'

Mum smiles and walks to Beth's room.

'Beth,' she says.

'They were here yesterday! They can't just—'

'We don't have ownership in this house, Beth. You know that. What's mine is yours and your's mine.'

This is code for Mum saying she had no clean clothes for her yoga class yesterday, so she took Beth's pants.

'I don't see Dad racing into Jesse's room to wear his shorts and t-shirt,' answers Beth.

'I don't mind if he does,' I venture.

'Shut up, Jesse.'

'Beth, we don't use such language in this house,' Mum's voice drips with patience.

'Fine. I'll walk outside and scream, "Shut up, Jesse",' Beth argues.

'You know what I mean, Beth. We're a,' Mum searches for the right word, 'a collective. We make decisions together. We share.'

I fear Mum and Dad haven't thought through this philosophy. Trevor and I can foresee the day Beth gets her driver's licence. She'll start demanding equal access to Mum's Volvo. Some serious readjustments will need to take place in the democracy of 12 Wellington Drive, Banksia.

Mum walks down the hallway into her bedroom and returns with the yoga pants. She tosses them into Beth's room without saying a word.

'They're dirty!' says Beth.

'They've been worn once.'

'No-one else at school has to share clothes with their mother,' says Beth. 'Crystal and Jade get to buy whatever they like at the shops.'

Beth's five best friends are Crystal, Jade, Ruby, Sapphire and Amber. If you have a rock for a name, you get to go to the shops whenever you like.

Beth can't go to the shops, as our family, the collective, has gardening duties every Saturday morning. I'm growing tomatoes from seeds. They're lined up on my bedroom window, waiting to grow. So far, one of the eleven pots has sprouted. Only it doesn't look like a seedling, more like fungus. Perhaps I've been watering them too much?

Beth is in charge of loose-leaf lettuce. She plants, she waters, she nourishes with Charlie Carp plant food, she pulls off dead leaves and she harvests. Mum tosses the lettuce leaves into a salad and, at dinner, she never fails to pat Beth on the wrist and say, 'We're eating the joys of Beth's labours'.

Beth has taken a vow of abstinence from all things green for the next few weeks. She says she wants to go on a black diet, which consists of Coca-Cola and charred meat.

Mum and Dad's gardening duties are the fruit trees and the watermelon patch. Dad's looking after the plum, pear and peach trees and Mum's tending the watermelon. Every morning, she feeds slices into the juicer, with ginger. She says it's good for blood pressure and circulation.

Dad's harvest hasn't been as successful. So far, we've eaten four plums which had a strange red-yellow flesh, but were tart and juicy. Beth pulled a face and threw her plum, half-eaten, into the bush next door. When Dad looked unhappy, Beth said she was making an offering to nature. Dad cheered up and suggested we all throw our seeds next door. I think he secretly hopes some more plum trees will grow. I saw a rat there yesterday, slinking around. I'm not sure a black rat is a native species, but he certainly looked well-fed.

'The least you can do is drive us to school,' Beth says. 'That way my pants won't get any dirtier walking.'

'Clothes don't just accumulate dirt from being worn, Beth.'

'Jesse's do!'

It's true. That's why I wear black. The kids at school are starting to think I'm an emo. When Hunter called me that on Friday, I thought he meant emu, so I corrected him.

'Emo the Emu!' yelled Hunter.

Everyone laughed.

Not because it was funny, of course. Simply because it came from the mouth of Hunter Riley. I've only been at school for three months, but I soon learned that Hunter is the class anarchist, law-breaker and the boy most likely to set the record for continuous lunchtime detentions. I've heard rumours of Hunter being suspended twice last year. Skye Delaney said he'd been caught smashing the heads off sunflowers with a golf club. Anastasia O'Brien said Hunter had been suspended for shaving Mrs Tomkin's cat. Skye said she'd heard her mum talking about neighbours' garden hoses being tied around the exhausts of parked cars. Everyone keeps away from Hunter, just in case.

A few weeks ago, Hunter came to school with a new haircut which I secretly called the starving mullet: mohawk on top, long at the back and shaved around the sides. He looked like a nature strip on the Benson Freeway. I didn't say this aloud. Making fun of Hunter is forbidden, in fear of atomic wedgies and twisted arms. Strictly speaking, making fun of anyone at school is not allowed, but Hunter does what he likes. And what he likes is being rude.

I expect to arrive in class today to be greeted with calls of 'Emo the Emu'. Which is better than my last nickname 'Jesus Freak'. All because I happened to mention religious instruction classes at my previous school.

I tried to explain about Trevor, but it was a losing battle. Now I know how the Mormons feel, walking from door to door, trying to get everyone to enlist and start worshipping their imaginary friend; trying to convince the world that Mormonism is more fun than watching television or playing football or having barbecues or swimming at the beach.

Trevor doesn't try to convert anyone. He just hangs there, on my wall, listening.

Beth walks out of her bedroom wearing the slightly worn yoga pants and a halter-neck top. Her hair is dyed purple-black and sweeps across the front of her face. She wears silver rings on most of her fingers and has been contemplating a nose-ring, but she hasn't told Mum and Dad yet. She's waiting for the right moment.

'Beth, you can't go to school dressed like that,' says Mum.

'In dirty clothes?' Beth answers.

'In a revealing outfit like that,' says Mum. Her voice drops to a whisper, 'Your bra straps are showing.'

'The only thing I'm *revealing* is that my parents are too stingy to buy me new underwear.' Beth walks out the front door before Mum can answer.

Mum looks at me. 'Jesse, can you tell your sister I'm not driving her to school dressed like that.'

'She'll just walk, Mum.'

'Well, so be it,' Mum responds.

That means I'll have to walk as well. I'm not showing any underwear. I'm tempted to pull my pants down a little, homeboy style, to display my boxers, but think better of it.

'Sorry, Jesse,' says Mum. 'I can't be a party to my daughter dressing like a teenage girl.'

'She is a teenage girl, Mum.'

'Don't be silly, Jesse. She's fourteen.' She starts to juice another slice of watermelon, for her blood pressure.

I trudge out the front door and am pleased to see it's stopped raining. Beth is standing beside the passenger door of the beat-up Volvo. She looks at me, hopefully. I shake my head.

Beth calls out, 'Fascist!' to the closed front door.

I follow her out the gate and down Wellington Drive. The clouds gather over Benson Freeway in the distance.

'Why is she so stubborn?' says Beth.

I shrug.

'Do these pants look really worn?' asks Beth.

'They look great, sis.'

Beth smiles. 'You're okay, Jesse. For somebody who talks to himself.'

'I'm philosoph … philsoph … I like to think aloud,' I say.

'That's fine, as long as you don't start hearing voices and weird—'

'Trevor doesn't talk, I told you. He's a …'

'Picture on the wall,' Beth suggests.

'Sounding board,' I counter.

'That's something Mum would say,' Beth grins.

'People talk to dogs and cats and horses and fish don't they?'

Beth nods.

'And everyone knows animals can't understand. Not really,' I add.

'Are you calling Jesus Christ our Saviour your pet?' Beth asks.

'No!' I blush uncontrollably at the image of the Mormons, Catholics and Salvos all lining up in our front yard when I'm home alone to try to force me to change my evil ways.

'Everybody needs someone,' I mumble.

As if on cue, standing at the intersection ahead is Ryan Blake. Ryan wears really tight jeans, large black riding boots and a stripy t-shirt. He looks like a hipster *Where's Wally*.

Beth immediately quickens her step. I get the message and slow down. When Beth reaches Ryan he puts his arm around her shoulder. His hand is touching her bra strap. I look away, in case I send negative vibes back home to Mum. She might do herself an injury while juicing the watermelon.

I look back. Beth and Ryan are now holding hands.

I follow at a safe younger brother distance.

And talk to myself.

2
HUNTER

Hunter Riley looks out the window. It's raining. Again. He quietly slides the window open and leans as far out as he dares. Raindrops wet his hair, roll down his cheeks and drop from his chin onto the corrugated iron roof. He closes his eyes and shakes his head, like a dog under a sprinkler.

From a gum tree near the fence comes the cackle of a kookaburra. Hunter opens his eyes, startled. He spies the bird in the highest branch. The kookaburra ruffles the rainwater from its feathers and opens its beak wide, as if yawning.

'At least you don't have to go to school,' Hunter says.

The kookaburra tilts its head and looks down into the garden. Hunter follows its gaze. A lizard scurries under a rock to safety. Hunter looks back at the bird. Their eyes meet.

'Ha!' says Hunter.

The rain falls steadily. Water streaks down Hunter's cheeks but he keeps his head out the window. The bird swoops along the roof line past Hunter and flaps away to a distant gum tree.

Hunter hears footsteps outside his door. He retreats into the room and climbs back into bed, rubbing his hair on the sheet.

He sees the doorhandle turn and quickly closes his eyes.

The door creaks. Hunter keeps his eyes closed, but knows his mum has entered the room. Ever since his dad left, she comes and looks at him sleeping. A raindrop runs down his cheek. In the quiet of the morning, he's sure he can hear her sigh. He keeps very still until she walks out of the room and gently closes the door.

After dressing into his school clothes of blue pants and a red skater shirt, Hunter walks downstairs. He stands at the kitchen doorway spying his mum sitting at the table. She stares at a bowl full of apples, oranges and pears. One banana sits on top, smiley faced. An ant crawls along the skin of the banana. She reaches toward the insect and with one finger blocks the ant's progress. The insect stops, then tentatively moves toward her long fingernail. She smiles. The ant creeps onto her finger. She stands and walks to the back door, opening it quietly.

Hunter walks into the kitchen and watches his mum on the back verandah. She leans down to a row of pot plants and places her finger close to the leaf of a basil plant.

'Everyone likes basil,' Mrs Riley says to the ant. She sighs and looks up at the rain still falling.

Hunter switches on the kettle for his mum's morning cup of tea. He scoops two spoonfuls of tea-leaves into the pot and when the jug boils, carefully pours the water to just below the spout. Enough for two cups, just the way Mum likes it.

He walks to the cupboard for a bowl and spoon, plonks them on the table and sits, reaching for the Weet-Bix and milk.

'Good morning, Hunter,' his mum says as she enters the kitchen.

Hunter spoons half a Weet-Bix into his mouth. 'It's Monday, how can it be a good morning,' he mumbles, a dribble of milk running down his chin. He doesn't bother to wipe and it drips back into his bowl.

'But you like school, dear.'

'Ha!'

'A boy should like school,' she adds.

'Ha!'

'Thanks for the tea,' she says. She takes a sip.

Hunter finishes his cereal. He looks at the packet

of Weet-Bix, considering. Instead of another helping, he picks up the bowl and carries it to the empty sink. He opens the fridge door and stares inside.

'I've packed your lunch box, Hunter. It's already in your bag.'

'Peanut butter?' he asks.

She nods. 'And an apple.'

Hunter closes the fridge door.

'Don't forget to clean your teeth,' she says.

'Why?'

'So you'll smell fresh.'

'I'm not kissing anyone!' he says.

'For dental hygiene, so your teeth won't fall out when you're old,' she says.

Hunter doesn't answer and walks back upstairs.

'Ha!' Mrs Riley says, to no-one in particular.

3
jesse

The five mudbrick buildings of Kawawill School nestle at the foot of a long bush track. Each of the buildings is painted a different shade of ochre. In the bush surrounding the school there are swings and cubbyhouses and a climbing gym. There is no sports oval. The only grass is in the central area between the buildings.

Students are dropped at the top of the hill by parents or buses and we wander four hundred metres down the track to the school grounds. At the end of the track is a sign with a 'Thought for the Day' hand-written on it.

This Monday morning, I'm standing in front of the sign. It reads:

Kind words are the easiest to speak.

A voice booms behind me, 'EMO!'

'Hi, Hunter,' I say, without bothering to turn around.

'Whoa! Emo the Emu has eyes in the back of his head.' Hunter slaps me on the shoulder. He reads the sign and then glances my way. 'That's bull. I can just as easily call you,' he looks at my clothes, 'the Black Assassin as I can call you Emo.'

'Or Jesse,' I suggest.

'Now why would I bother calling you by your real name, Darkman?'

'Hunter, you are an endless font of meaningless names,' I say.

'You said it, Bleakboy.' Hunter looks me up and down once more, as if he's storing away another twenty nicknames for lunchtime, then he walks into Doris.

I don't mean he walks into a person called Doris. Doris is the name of the administration building, in honour of the founder of our school Doris Leadmeir. The primary building is Arnold, named after Doris's husband, who designed the school layout. Doris and Arnold, the people, are both long dead, but the buildings live on. The other buildings are: Edith, the kindergarten building (Edith Bricknell was the first kindy teacher); Lillian, the high school building (Lillian Roche was the woman who donated land for the school to be built on); and finally, Walter, the toilet

16

block (Walter C Cuthbert was the first school janitor).

The teachers tell us to use the names of the buildings, to remember the founders. The school doesn't have a principal. Each year, one of the staff is elected by their fellow teachers as the team coordinator. This year it's Larry Ames. Teachers must be addressed by their first name. Larry, never Mr Ames.

And here he is now. Larry walks up the path, wearing three-quarter length bushwalking pants and a 'Greenpeace' t-shirt. He's also wearing sandals, which, strictly speaking, students are discouraged from wearing. Because of snakes. Larry isn't scared.

He stands in front of the sign, takes off his floppy hat and bangs it against his knee, as if a nest of spiders is hiding under the brim.

'Hi, Larry.'

'G'day, Jesse.' He nods at the sign. 'That's my slogan. Pretty good, hey?' He doesn't wait for an answer as he heads off to the high school. Sorry, I mean Lillian.

Suddenly, dance music blares over the PA system, which means it's time to go to class. Each month, a different class gets to choose the music. This month it's year four. Next month it's year nine, so I'm hoping for a serious headbanging metal attack. I'm not sure how Larry will respond. He may write a 'Thought for the Day' to counteract all the harsh vibes the music will give out.

'Hi, Jesse,' says Kate, a girl in my class with curly black hair and braces.

'Hi, Kate. Thanks for not calling me Emo.'

Kate looks around quickly for Hunter before leaning close and whispering, 'Hunter is a turnip.' Kate adds, 'Did you do your personal assessment tasks?'

That's what we're supposed to call homework.

'Yep. I read a book on the bell frog and drew a picture of it. What was your topic?'

'Whales.' Kate winks. 'I've taken a slightly different approach.' She leads me into our classroom in Arnold and we take our seats near the front. The rest of the class are already seated, except Hunter. He's sitting on the window ledge. He makes a gloomy sound at the back of his throat when I walk in, like the theme music to a horror movie.

He's about to say something when Sarah, our teacher, walks in.

'Good morning, Class 6S,' she says.

'Good morning, Sarah,' we respond together, except Hunter. He times his greeting to be half-a-second behind, like an echo.

Sarah flashes him a tired look and he slowly sits down on his chair. She stands in front of the class and says, 'Okay. Let's have a selection of readings from your personal assessment tasks.'

I raise my hand.

'Yes, Jesse.'

'I didn't write anything, Ms, I mean Sarah. I just drew something.'

Sarah smiles. 'No worries. We'll have a selection of readings and displays of your tasks. Who wants to start?'

Everyone raises their hands, except Hunter and me.

'Anastasia first,' says Sarah. She walks to the side window and leans against the ledge, facing into the room. She smiles at Anastasia, who stands and picks up her glasses from her desk. She puts them on before reading her story. Her voice is distant and rhythmic, like the sound of a train going over a bridge.

Anastasia's story is about a girl finding an injured marsupial bilby in the bush and nursing it back to health. In the story, the main character is called Anastasia and she learns how to communicate with the bilby. They live together in the forest and eat mushrooms and mangoes. One day while foraging for food, they meet a handsome young man called Justin B.

Anastasia blushes, before continuing with the story.

Justin B is a reclusive pop star who's made his home in the forest to escape the thousands of young girls who scream outside his Malibu apartment. Together, Anastasia and Justin B write a song called 'One less lonely bilby'.

When Anastasia finishes her story, everyone applauds, except Hunter who coughs loudly.

Sarah looks up. 'Are you all right, Hunter?'

Hunter grins. 'I think I need to go to Walter.'

Sarah nods and Hunter walks out of the room, singing, 'I'm off to Walter, Walter the toilet block'.

'That's enough, Hunter,' Sarah calls after him.

'No worries, Sarah.'

He's left the door open. Without thinking, I get up to close it.

'Thanks, Jesse.'

'That's okay, Sarah. Can I lock it as well?' The class giggles, but Sarah smiles and says, 'We're inclusive, remember Jesse?'

'Would you like to go next, Kate?' asks Sarah.

Kate stands and confidently walks to the front of the room. She looks at everyone in the class, smiling at me, and in a loud voice, begins, 'My story is about whales'.

'Ooh, they're so beautiful,' says Skye, from the second row.

Kate ignores her. 'Whales are mammals that live in the ocean. They range in size from the giant blue whale to the much smaller pygmy sperm whale.' Kate looks up at Sarah. Sarah nods.

Kate continues, 'The common minke whale is the main species hunted and killed by Japanese and Norwegian whalers. Hundreds are slaughtered every year.'

'SARAH!' yells Skye.

'Whale meat is high in protein and is lower in calories than beef and pork. It also has a much higher iron content and is rich in—'

'Kate?' Sarah's voice is quiet.

Kate stops reading and looks at the teacher.

Skye starts sobbing, although I suspect she's just pretending.

'I thought the personal assessment task I designed,' Sarah says, 'was for us to appreciate the gift of nature. You appear to be talking about eating a—'

'Beautiful animal!' Skye interrupts.

Sarah takes a deep breath. 'Skye. Remember our guidelines about calling out in class.'

'But she's eating whales,' Skye responds.

'Not in class she's not.' Sarah shifts her focus to Kate. 'May I ask why you chose this topic, Kate?'

At this very moment, Hunter walks in and strolls past Kate.

'Some animals—' Kate starts.

'Who you calling an animal?' Hunter turns and interrupts.

'We were talking about whales,' says Sarah, waiting a few crucial seconds before adding, 'not you.'

The class laughs.

Hunter scowls at us all, trying to pick who he'll pay back at lunchtime. I almost burst a lung holding my breath to stop giggling. But his eyes settle on me.

'I love whales,' Kate looks meaningfully at Skye, 'but they're eaten by native communities in Norway and Canada.'

'And the Japanese?' Sarah asks.

Kate smiles. 'Actually, Sarah, whale meat is eaten in Japanese schools.'

The class shudders as one. Our canteen, housed at the back of Lillian, serves only vegetarian food. Monday's speciality is tofu burgers.

'You haven't really answered my question, Kate,' continues Sarah, her voice taking on some of the Skye-anguish. 'Why did you choose this topic?'

'Animals are eaten, whether we like it or not.' Kate looks toward the class for support. Everyone looks away except me. 'Even beautiful animals like whales and fur seals.'

This is too much for Skye. She scrapes back her chair and runs out of the room, doing a Hunter and leaving the door open; open and gaping like a wound in a minke whale caused by a harpoon.

Kate continues, as if she's read my mind. 'The traditional native hunters use harpoons—'

'Okay, that's enough.' Sarah walks quickly toward Kate. 'Kate, I appreciate your alternative view of the beauty and gift of nature, but perhaps I'll read your personal assessment task alone at lunchtime.'

'Make sure you've eaten first, Sarah,' suggests Hunter.

Sarah ignores him, takes the paper from Kate and ushers her back to her seat. She asks Eoin to stand and read to the class.

Eoin stands *on* his chair.

Everyone laughs. He looks around the room, smiling.

'Why are you standing on your chair, Eoin?' asks Sarah.

'My dad says soundwaves carry further if they aren't interrupted by stuff.'

'Thank you for the physics lesson, Eoin. Your dad is correct, but let's just stand on the floor, shall we?' Sarah looks sternly at Lance in the back row, who is still giggling. Lance coughs once and falls silent.

'You may begin, Eoin,' says Sarah.

'My story is about a boy called Eoin who lives with the chimpanzees of Africa. Eoin learns to talk to the chimps and they swing from tree to tree in the jungle. Eoin builds a treehouse high in the forest ...'

And so it goes until lunchtime. The gift of nature.

And then tofu burgers.

4
HUNTER

It's lunchtime and Hunter is in the boys toilet block, again. He looks into the mirror and smiles.

'Walter,' he says to himself. 'What a stupid name.'

A year two boy walks in. He looks at Hunter and says, 'Pardon?'

'Think of a name,' Hunter says.

The boy looks behind him, not sure if Hunter is talking to him.

'A name. Any name,' repeats Hunter.

'Samuel,' the boy says.

'That's your name, isn't it?'

The boy nods.

'Okay, Mr Original, think of another name.'

Samuel shuffles from one foot to the other. He needs to go to the toilet. 'Ralph,' he says.

'Your dog's name, right?' says Hunter.

Samuel can't hold on much longer. He nods and takes a step toward the cubicle.

'One more name,' says Hunter.

Samuel feels his bottom lip wobbling. He looks at his shoes and notices one lace is untied. He mumbles, 'Hunter.'

'You want to name the toilet block after me?' Hunter grins.

'No! I didn't mean ... Pete!' Samuel suggests.

Hunter laughs. 'Pete, the place to pee!'

Samuel walks toward the cubicle.

'The toilet's broken,' Hunter says.

Samuel's face goes red. He can't hold on. He bites his top lip and tries to think of something other than his overriding need to pee.

'You can use the girls toilet,' Hunter says.

Samuel takes a step backward, then stops and says, 'But ... but what if there's a girl?'

'Close your eyes,' Hunter says. Samuel rushes out of Walter. Hunter can hear his hurried footsteps, next door in the girls toilet. Then over the partition, 'I only want to wee!'

Hunter smiles. He looks at his reflection and rubs his hand through his hair. Time for a new haircut.

He checks his watch. Ten minutes before lunch finishes. He thinks back to the class discussion on whales and wonders if Kate was making a joke about him. What was she saying while he was at Walter?

The only way to find out is to ask Jesse. That new kid can't tell a lie. Hunter will force it out of him, if he has to.

Hunter ambles around the schoolyard, on the lookout for Jesse. He's probably playing with some of the younger kids, Hunter imagines. Such a sonk.

'Hunter,' an adult voice comes from behind.

Hunter keeps walking.

'Hunter!' The voice is more demanding.

Hunter turns around.

'Didn't you hear me the first time, Hunter?' says Larry.

Hunter shrugs.

'Well, that's not the issue,' says Larry. A group of year nine girls walk between the two of them. Larry motions to the bench seat, under the pine trees. Hunter follows, reluctantly. Larry sits down. Hunter remains standing.

'I've had a complaint,' says Larry. 'From a ... well, it doesn't matter who it's from. There's a rumour that Walter is defective.' Larry looks toward the kindy kids playing on the climbing equipment. 'Do you know where this could have started, Hunter?'

'Yep, Larry. It was me,' Hunter admits.

Larry had been expecting denials. 'This is very serious, Hunter.'

'I know, Larry.'

Larry scratches his beard. 'The young boy in

question, could have had an unfortunate … accident. If you get my meaning.'

'Absolutely,' says Hunter.

'I must say, Hunter, I didn't expect you to admit to such behaviour,' says Larry.

'I'm proud to, Larry.'

'Proud!'

'You bet. Just imagine what would have happened if I hadn't stopped the boy from using the toilet.'

Larry looks aghast. 'I'm sorry?'

'The toilet, Larry. It was broken. I saved the boy from getting soaked.'

'That's … that's not what I understood.' Larry stares at Hunter. 'I've just come from Walter, Hunter. All the toilets appear to be working fine.'

'I know, Larry. After I stopped the boy, Samuel I think his name was, I spent five minutes jiggling with the toilet, fixing it.'

'Well … how am I,' Larry stammers.

'Don't worry, Larry. It's free. I wouldn't dream of charging the school. I'm just glad Samuel let you know of the incident.'

Music starts. Disco Inferno. There are a few minutes until the end of lunchtime. Larry doesn't move. Hunter elaborately checks his watch. 'I'd better go, Larry. I want to borrow a library book.'

Larry nods and watches Hunter stride away.

Hunter can barely contain his laughter.

5

Jesse

I'm scrunched down as low as possible on a beanbag in the library, the smallest room in Edith. I'm holding the largest book I can find to offer myself the most camouflage. Hunter is probably on the warpath and in his sights are not whales, fur seals, bilbies or chimpanzees.

I almost burst my lungs trying not to laugh in class and look where it's got me. Luckily, the words 'library' and 'Hunter' rarely mix, so I snuggle down and contemplate the nutritional value of whales. Yep, Kate did nothing but repeat the information that can be found in our own library. If Sue, the librarian, only knew what was on her shelves.

Whale meat is low in cholesterol. I wonder if I should tell Dad. The only animals we eat at home are fish and free-range chicken. At least once a week, over dinner, Dad says, 'We steer clear of red meat in this house'. Then he waits for us all to laugh at the pun. No-one does.

'Get it, *steer*.' He chomps on his wild Atlantic salmon, satisfied he's fulfilled his father-humour quota for the week. Sometimes, Mum joins in. 'No bull, dear,' she titters. If we were a normal family, we'd be eating dinner in front of the television, so Beth and I could concentrate on *Home and Away* and ignore this comedy double bill.

'Good one, Faith,' says Dad. 'There's no kowtowing in this house.'

This is obviously nonsensical, but it brings a huge laugh from Dad. He's on a roll now. He looks across the table at me. 'You don't have a beef with our humour do you, son?'

Luckily my mouth is too full of wild Atlantic salmon to answer.

'May I be excused?' asks Beth.

'You want to be alone, Beth,' he says, 'to stew in your own juices!' Dad almost falls off the chair, he's laughing so much. Beth looks at me and rolls her eyes.

'Anthony, stop ribbing our daughter,' adds Mum.

What on earth has possessed these people? Is the salmon contaminated with mercury causing imme-diate brain damage? Mum reaches across the table and pats Beth's wrist. 'Sorry, Beth. You can go as soon as you've finished eating.'

Beth scoffs her food at a furious rate and takes her plate across to the sink.

A shadow passes over the beanbag.

'You seem engrossed in that book, Jesse James Jones,' says Sue, the librarian.

I nod.

Sue sits in the opposite beanbag. She takes off her glasses and cleans them on her 'Books before Bombs' t-shirt. She's wearing loose-fitting trousers, with a wide belt that has a Harry Potter buckle, the slash mark on his face prominent.

'What's it about?' she asks.

'Animals,' I answer.

'Don't tell me about animals,' she laughs.

Have you ever noticed when someone says, 'Don't tell me about', it means they're going to give you a twenty-minute lecture on what they just told you not to tell them about?

'We've got a veritable zoo at home. Cats, dogs, budgies, sheep, a pig called—'

'Babe?' I interrupt.

'How did you guess, Jesse? And cows, lots of chickens, even a few geese and ducks,' Sue says.

As she's talking, I flip through the pages to D for duck. Yep, duck is the national dish of France. She really should take care with the books on display.

'My husband and I run a rescue service for animals,' Sue adds.

For some reason, I picture her in a lifesaver's uniform running into the ocean to rescue a pig that's fallen off a surfboard. The pig is floundering in the fast-moving rip, one trotter held aloft as it feebly attempts to snort for help. Sue, a surf ski under her arm, dives into the waves, jumps on the board and paddles to where Babe was last seen.

'Did you hear what I said, Jesse?' Sue asks.

'Yeah. No. Sorry?'

'You can visit if you like. We have lots of animals to feed. Babe would love to meet you. He's such a friendly pig.'

Hunter is standing beside the entrance to the library, peering through the window. The window fogs up with his breath and I slink lower into the beanbag. Thank Trevor, he didn't see me.

'You have a customer,' I whisper to Sue.

She looks around as Hunter walks through the door. 'Hello, Hunter. We were just talking about pigs.'

It really is Hunter's day for being compared to animals. Hunter snorts and walks away, not even bothering to answer Sue.

'Sorry about Hunter, Sue,' I say. 'He's a little upset, since his pet goldfish died.' I can't resist adding, 'Maybe you should invite him to your farm. He'd love

31

to meet Babe.' I get up to leave. 'But don't mention the fish, okay? He's trying to …'

'Move on?' Sue suggests.

I nod and wave from the doorway, careful as I step into the corridor that Hunter isn't lurking.

6

HUNTER

Hunter stands on the corner of Lister and Brighton Streets, looking across at the football oval and the young players running laps. He thinks of his father and how years ago, he'd wait expectantly for his dad to come to football training. Ha! Hunter remembers looking at the car park instead of the football, his coach blowing the whistle to get his attention. Only once in the two years Hunter played footy did his dad turn up to training. And even then he spent most of the time on his mobile phone. He never made the Saturday game. Work. As if that one word was excuse enough. And then his father left home for good.

Hunter sighs and carries his bag to the fountain in Elkhorn Park. He watches the young woman in trackpants and sweatshirt punching the gloves of her personal trainer. She skips from foot to foot and throws a punch with a loud exhalation of breath. Droplets of sweat fly from her forehead with every punch she throws. Hunter hopes her personal trainer can revive heart attack victims. The trainer signals a break and the woman rests on her haunches. The trainer offers her a water bottle. She drinks it quickly, water spilling down her shirt.

'Hey, leave me alone,' a voice calls from the opposite side of the park. It's Samuel, the boy from the toilet. He's reaching for his backpack which is being swung in the air by Watson Watts, from year five.

Watson towers over Samuel and gloats, 'Come on, you can do better than that'. Samuel jumps up and nearly grabs the strap, but Watson pulls it away, just in time. Samuel swings his arm at Watson, who easily dodges it. Then, Samuel crosses his arms and waits. Watson swings the bag a few more times and flings it onto the grass, a few metres away. The boys look at each other, neither moving.

'It's all yours,' Watson says.

Samuel takes a deep breath, looks around the park for help, sees no-one but Hunter at the fountain and decides to make a run for it. He sprints toward the bag, but Watson overtakes him and scoops it up with one deft movement. Samuel falls to the grass and starts to cry.

Hunter notices Watson is holding only one bag: Samuel's. He scans the park and sees Watson's bag on the bus-shelter seat. 'Ha!' He walks casually over to the shelter. The name tag reads, 'Watson Watts'. What a stupid name, Hunter thinks. He picks up the bag and walks toward the boys. Samuel sees Hunter first. He buries his head in his hands, afraid of what's going to happen next.

'Hunter!' calls Watson. It takes him a minute to notice that Hunter is carrying two bags and one of them is his.

Hunter turns to Samuel instead of Watson. 'Hey, Samuel,' says Hunter, his voice flat and quiet. 'Which bag do you want?' Hunter holds Watson's bag in front of him. 'This one, or yours?'

'That's mine,' says Watson.

Hunter and Samuel ignore him. Samuel points to his own bag, still in Watson's grip. 'Mine,' he says. 'Please.'

Hunter stares at Watson. Watson looks furtively around the park. The woman and her personal trainer are jogging away, heading toward the path along the creek.

'We were just having fun, weren't we, Samuel?' says Watson.

'No,' says Samuel.

'Come on, Hunter, it's just a game,' says Watson, his voice uncertain.

An old man drives slowly along the path on his mobility scooter, his shopping in the basket on the handlebars. He wears a peaked cap and has a pipe in his mouth, the smoke trailing behind, like a faulty exhaust. He slows down when he passes the boys.

Watson says, 'Hey.'

The old man stops his cart. He takes the pipe out of his mouth. 'Can I help you?' he says, in a deep voice.

Hunter smiles. 'No, thank you, sir. Watto thought he recognised you, that's all.'

The old man looks at Samuel on the grass. Samuel nods his head. Watson swallows hard and doesn't say a word. The old man puts his pipe back into his mouth and takes a slow puff, before driving away.

Once the man is out of hearing range, Watson chucks Samuel's bag on the grass. Samuel jumps up, gathers the bag and runs past Hunter to the path beside the creek.

Watson looks at the ground and says, 'Can I have my bag, Hunter?'

Hunter waits until Samuel is out of sight.

'Come on, Watto.' He smiles. 'You can do better than that.'

7
jesse

On the way home from school, Kate catches up to me at the street corner. She's whistling a slow mournful sound. We don't speak until she finishes.

'That sounded so sad,' I say.

Kate smiles. 'It's the mating call of the humpback whale.'

'A live humpback whale,' I add.

Kate giggles. 'Skye is such a ...'

'Stresshead?' I suggest.

'Blubber guts! And I don't mean whale blubber either.' Kate looks at me. 'You were the only one who understood, Jesse.'

I nod.

'I thought Sarah would get it,' Kate says.

'Teachers are scared of tears,' I say.

'I was going to suggest we all write protest letters

to the Japanese Embassy.' Kate smiles. 'I thought we could save the whales and get out of maths in the same afternoon.'

'Algebra makes my brain hurt,' I say.

'The only good thing about maths is watching Hunter squirm in his seat all afternoon,' Kate adds.

'How many times can one boy go to Walter?' I say.

'Maybe his bladder and brain are connected,' Kate says.

'Yeah, and they're both leaking,' I respond.

Kate laughs. 'Is that toilet humour?'

She stops walking and takes off her backpack. She rummages inside and brings out her notebook. 'Do you have a pen, Jesse?'

I reach into the side pocket of my backpack and take out a pen, handing it to her. On a scrap of paper, Kate writes something and gives it to me, along with my pen.

'The Japanese Embassy?' I ask, stuffing it in my pocket.

'Of course,' she says.

'I'll write soon,' I say. I wonder what Trevor would think about saving the whales. I'm sure he'd support it. Then, as usual, the next thought I have is if Trevor really supported the whales, he'd have a word ... upstairs ... to God.

'What are you thinking about, Jesse?' Kate asks.

I swallow hard. Kate never called me Jesus Freak last week, when Hunter turned on me.

'You could ask somebody else,' my voice is quiet, 'to stop the whaling.'

Kate nods. 'I've already sent letters to the Norwegian and Canadian Embassies.'

'No, I mean ...' I look up into the sky.

Kate notices. 'You mean ...' She points a finger to the heavens.

'It can't hurt,' I say.

Kate shrugs. 'I imagine if he,' she giggles to herself, 'or she is up there, they'd have more important things to do.'

'Like stopping wars?' I suggest.

'Yeah.' Kate punches me on the arm. 'Or stopping themselves from falling out of the sky. Why do people always look up for God?'

'Maybe he floats like a hot air balloon,' I suggest.

'He or she definitely doesn't sit on a cloud. I've been on a plane heaps of times and clouds don't look heavy enough to hold somebody as important as ...' She points skyward again.

'My parents tell me not to worship false gods,' I admit.

'My mum says the only supernatural thing in the universe is,' Kate touches her heart, 'inside us. It's what we do that counts.'

'But who makes us do it?' I ask.

Kate laughs. 'Dad says it's all nonsense and everyone knows the only true God plays in the midfield for Barcelona.'

We stop walking as we reach Elkhorn Park. Hunter is swinging a schoolbag wildly around his head. Watson is trying to grab it off Hunter, who holds him at bay with one outstretched hand.

'Hey!' Kate yells.

Hunter slows down his swinging and Watson manages to grab the bag. Both boys pull. Watson stumbles to his knees, but holds onto the bag. Hunter lets go of the strap and walks toward us. Behind him, Watson clutches the bag and hurries away. Without meaning to, I tighten the grip on my backpack.

'Bleakboy and Whale-eater,' says Hunter.

I look nervously toward Kate, wondering how she'll react. She doesn't say a word. I follow her example and we both stand silently a few metres from Hunter.

His glance wanders to my Dunlop Volleys. 'My uncle wears shoes like that,' he says. 'Old-man tennis shoes.'

He looks from Kate to me. 'You couldn't hit a tennis ball if you tried, Bleakboy.'

There's really nothing I can say to respond, so I bite my lip. Kate stifles a yawn. When it's obvious neither of us is going to react, Hunter starts looking uncomfortable. His eyes flit from Kate to me, looking for something else to pick on.

Kate smiles.

'How do you eat so much blubber with railway tracks on your teeth,' Hunter says.

Kate stops smiling. I think her braces give Kate an infectious smile, but I've never said that to her.

'You'd better not walk too close to a magnet with all that metal in your mouth.' Hunter mimics being drawn into a wall face first. He calls out, in a deliberately muffled voice, 'I'm stuck, I'm stuck!'

I can hear Kate's teeth grinding with the effort to remain silent.

Hunter looks scornfully at both of us. 'Talking to you two is like talking to a wall,' he says. 'A metal wall.'

Kate yawns, this time not hiding her mouth with her hand. Both sets of braces are showing. She glances toward me and tilts her head, indicating we should leave. She turns away from Hunter. A second later, I do the same. At the far end of the park, Watson is about to board a bus home, both hands clutching his backpack.

Hunter calls from behind us, 'Bleakboy and Whale-eater.' His voice echoes across the park until we cross the road. I sneak a glance back and see Hunter standing alone wondering where Watson has gone and wondering what to do next.

Kate says, 'It works!'

'Pardon?'

'Mum told me about non-violent protest.' Kate frowns. 'I think that's what she called it. She said the best thing to do when somebody picks on you is nothing.'

'Somebody should tell Watson,' I suggest.

'Hunter didn't know what to do,' says Kate.

'Yeah, but ...' I don't want to say the obvious.

'But what?'

'If I was here alone, just boy against boy, Hunter would have been swinging my backpack, not Watson's,' I say.

Kate shakes her head. 'You'll never know until you try it.'

I giggle. 'You mean I should offer myself to Hunter? To pick on?'

Kate punches my arm lightly again. 'We have the power, Jesse.'

I rub my arm. 'No. I have old-man tennis shoes.' We both look down. 'And Hunter has the muscles,' I add.

Kate just smiles and taps a finger to the side of her head as if to say brains beat brawn.

8
HUNTER

On the long walk home, Hunter stops at the intersection of Ficus and Burnley Streets. He looks east along Ficus Street to where Saint Stephen's Church is surrounded by a stone wall and flowering shrubs. That's where his parents got married. His mum told him it was a perfect summer's day and they took photos under a wattle tree in bloom.

And then the wasps flew down from the tree and stung the bridesmaids, the groom, the best man and most of the wedding party. Everyone except the bride and the photographer. The wedding album at home is packed with photos of people slapping themselves. The reception was held at the local conference centre and instead of passing around glasses of champagne, they shared ointment for the bites. Everyone was red and blotchy, except Hunter's mum. His father had swollen lips for days, Mum said. He could barely speak and they couldn't kiss. Hunter liked that story.

The old man on the scooter from the park pulls up alongside Hunter. He reaches into his pocket for a box of matches to light his pipe and cups one hand around the flame. He puffs and Hunter smells the acrid smoke. Hunter waits for him to move on, but he doesn't. He just sits on the scooter looking down the street.

'I used to walk to the shops every day,' the old man says, more to himself than Hunter. 'Now I drive this contraption, like an invalid.' Hunter notices the shopping in the basket: pasta, tinned sauce, a bottle of milk and dog food.

'What sort of dog do you have?' Hunter asks.

The old man laughs. 'One that doesn't yap all night. One that knows when to sit at my feet and,' the old man takes a puff, 'when to leave me alone.' He reaches into the shopping basket and holds up the tin of dog food. 'Deefer doesn't need much.' He drops the tin back in the basket. 'We both eat out of tins.'

'Deefer? What sort of name is that?' Hunter says.

'D for dog. Deefer,' chuckles the old man. 'Something easy to remember.' He taps one finger against his temple. 'In case I start losing my marbles as well as my mobility.'

'Where's your wife?' Hunter asks.

The old man looks sharply at Hunter. He studies his pipe for a few seconds before answering, 'She's passed on'. He holds up the pipe. 'They say this thing will kill me.' He scoffs. 'It's the heart that kills us in the end. One way or another.' The old man coughs into his handkerchief. 'All the same, laddie, I wouldn't be taking it up if I were you. The smell scares away the ladies!' He reaches down and taps the smouldering contents out onto the grass. 'Step on that for me, will you?'

Hunter walks around the scooter and presses the ash into the grass with his shoe.

'Was I interrupting something,' the old man says, 'back there in the park?'

Hunter shakes his head.

They both stare down Ficus Street. The wind suddenly picks up from the east. Storm clouds colour the horizon. A flock of starlings swoop across the sky, like a mottled fan unfolding. A soft-drink truck pulls up a few metres in front of them. The driver jumps down from his cabin and lifts a yellow plastic crate of assorted drinks from the tray top, carrying it into the house with a green-painted fence.

'When I was a kid,' the old man says, 'a bloke around the corner drove one of those trucks.' He looks cheekily at Hunter. 'He kept crate loads of soft drinks under his house.' The old man winks. 'Whenever I got thirsty, I knew just where to go. Even now, I can hardly resist the desire to just scoot alongside the truck, reach in, grab a bottle and be on my way.'

Hunter laughs at the image of a pensioner thief puttering away on his scooter. 'I'll keep watch, if you want,' he says.

The old man chuckles. 'We'd never make it, laddie. The battery on this thing is on its last legs. Much like me.'

The truck driver comes out from the house, carrying an empty crate. He pulls the tarp over the full crates on the tray top and ties it down with rope, ready for the approaching storm.

The old man turns his scooter, preparing to cross the road. 'I never ride down this side of Ficus,' he says. 'Going that close to the church gives me the screaming willies.' He waves the pipe at Hunter and speeds across the road. Hunter watches him reach the other side and scoot up the gutter, the food in the basket shaking, the old man intently holding the handlebars as he surges forward.

Hunter turns away and walks slowly down Burnley Street. Lightning forks in the distance. He practises spitting between the gap in his teeth, first for distance, then for accuracy. He's an expert by the time he reaches his house.

Hunter sits on his front fence, watching the storm bruise the horizon. A curtain of rain folds toward him. He hears the rain on the corrugated roof of Mrs Betts's house before he feels it. He closes his eyes and turns his face to the sky. Pock. Pock. Pock. The raindrops drum on his forehead, soak his hair and channel down his back. He opens his mouth to catch the drops and says, 'I'm eating the rain.' He giggles.

Hunter remembers when he was five years old, being caught in a thunderstorm with his dad. How his dad lifted a newspaper above their heads as they scurried for cover. They were soaked before reaching the safety of a bus shelter. While he watched the rain gush down the gutters and turn potholes into puddles, his father read the wet newspaper, peeling each page away from the other. Hunter marvelled at the sky, amazed that clouds could hold that much water. With one of his father's discarded sheets of newspaper, Hunter fashioned a boat: a newsprint canoe. He stepped from the shelter and launched it in the gutter. It swept away, riding the stormwater waves. Hunter knelt on the footpath and laughed. His father told him to come out of the rain.

A car horn sounds and Hunter opens his eyes, startled. Mrs Betts is pulling into her driveway. He hops off the fence and rushes across the road to where his neighbour is about to get out of her car. Hunter calls, 'I'll do it, Mrs Betts.' He quickly reaches over the gate and unlatches it, pushing it wide. He stands back as she drives through into the garage. He closes the gate and runs back across the road to his home. Mrs Betts waves in thanks.

Hunter leaps across his front fence and looks at the gutters, gushing wildly. If only he had a newspaper.

9

jesse

The problem with the internet is one moment I'm learning all about the campaign to stop the Japanese killing whales in the Southern Ocean and within two clicks, I'm staring at a starving boy from Ethiopia.

His name is Kelifa. He's eight years old and lives with his dad and four sisters. His mum died giving birth to his youngest sister, Mubina, last year. He looks at me with sad eyes from the computer screen. The cursor hovers over the 'DONATE NOW' button in the bottom right-hand corner. My hand shakes on the mouse. Anybody with four sisters deserves all the help I can offer.

I've checked my piggy bank and I have exactly nine dollars and sixty cents. If split six ways with his sisters and dad, that amounts to one dollar and sixty cents each. Which is not even enough to give him clean drinking water. My eyes wander to the water bottle on my desk. If only I could push the bottle through the screen and all the way to Kelifa in Africa.

I look out the window. The storm has cleared and Dad is tending his peach tree in the garden. He sees me watching and waves, then plucks a ripe peach from the tree. He tosses it into the air and catches it before taking a big bite. The juice spurts into his eye. He laughs and walks robot-like around the garden, his arms reaching out in front of him, feeling the way, pretending to be blind. Then he opens his eyes and takes another bite.

I wonder if hunger can cause real blindness. Kelifa appears to nod from his village in my computer. My throat is dry. Absentmindedly, I reach for the water bottle. But Kelifa is watching. I get up from my desk and walk down the hallway, taking a guilty drink as I go.

On the kitchen table is Dad's wallet, a twenty-dollar bill poking out.

I glance down the hall to my bedroom. Trevor looks blankly at me, through the doorway, his arms spread as if to say, 'It's your decision, Jesse'.

Mum and Beth are out shopping for groceries. In thirty minutes they'll arrive home and Mum will complain that she spent over two hundred dollars at the supermarket as she stores cans of food in the pantry. I doubt Kelifa has ever seen a pantry.

I quickly open Dad's wallet and take out his MasterCard. Running down the hallway, I avert my eyes from Trevor. 'Forgive me, Trev,' I whisper.

Kelifa is waiting. He looks thinner than a few minutes ago. I click on the 'DONATE NOW' button. A screen appears with all the details I need to fill in: name, address, card number, expiry date. I do it as quickly as my shaking hands allow.

My finger hovers over the mouse. One click and fifty dollars is on its way to Kelifa and his family. I hope his sisters share.

I hear the crunch of car wheels on gravel in the driveway. Beth's voice is loud, 'One chocolate bar!' I lean across and close my window.

My right index finger clicks the mouse.

Kelifa smiles.

10

HUNTER

The house echoes with emptiness when Hunter closes the front door. He walks to the kitchen and hangs his schoolbag on the hook. There's a personal assessment task in the bag and that's where it's staying. He opens the fridge door and reaches inside for a handful of grapes. When his mother brings them home from the supermarket, she pulls each grape from the stalk, and puts the fruit in a bowl, to encourage Hunter to eat them. As he crunches down on the skin, he wonders how far he could spit a grape. He closes the fridge door and notices the puddle he's created on the kitchen floor. He walks into the laundry and takes off his jeans, socks and t-shirt, tossing the squelchy bundle into the laundry basket.

He runs to his bedroom, where the blinds are rattling in the wind. He left the window open this morning. Hunter slams the window shut and looks out to the road, slick with damp. The storm has passed but the gutters are still surging. He wonders if the old man made it home in time. He tries to remember if the scooter had a roof.

Hunter leaves his bedroom and walks up the hallway to the closed door of the second bedroom. He reaches for the doorknob and a sudden clap of thunder booms in the distance. He quickly removes his hand from the knob.

'Ha!'

Even though he's only wearing undies, Hunter is sweating as he turns the handle and opens the door. In the corner is a single bed, covered with a doona. A pile of pillows is scattered along the bed, like a sleeping figure, round and pudgy. Next to the bed is a dresser and beside that are cardboard boxes, stacked three high. The weight of the boxes is forcing the bottom carton to sag and the stack looks about to fall at any moment. Hunter walks in and shoves the stack tight against the wall. Scrawled across the lid of the top box in his father's handwriting is the single word: 'Charity'.

He rips the masking tape off the box and reaches inside. He pulls out a long-sleeved business shirt, white with thin blue stripes, and holds it up to his nose. It smells of camphor mothballs and faint traces of his father's aftershave. He reaches into the box again and pulls out another shirt. And another. All white, with pinstripes. He wonders why his mother keeps all this stuff. Why his father didn't take it to the charity shop before he left.

On the opposite wall is a full-length mirror. Hunter goes to the window and looks down the street. No sign of his mother. He checks his watch. Thirty minutes until she arrives home from work. He puts his arms into his father's shirt and pulls it on, slowly fastening each button, leaving the top one undone. The shirt hangs down a little too far. Quickly he searches in the box for a pair of his father's slacks. Sure enough, at the bottom, neatly folded, are a few pairs. He pulls the dark blue pants up over his waist. They're baggy and too long. Hunter leans down and rolls up the cuffs before searching in the box to find a leather belt, frayed at the edges. He threads it through the belt loops and tightens it as far as it'll go. He takes a deep breath and stands in front of the mirror.

He looks like a ragdoll with a scowling face. He tries to smile, but it turns out all crooked and forced. Hunter stares at himself for a long time, looking for any resemblance to his father. He has brown eyes and olive skin, like his mum. Nothing like his father's blue eyes and pale skin. Hunter stands straighter, with his shoulders pulled back. His dad always leaned forward, as if he were trying to sell you something, as if he wanted to be your friend.

The fabric of the shirt itches at his neck and is clammy against his skin. He puts his hands in between the buttons and rips off the shirt. The buttons fly across the room, bouncing off the mirror. He unbuckles the belt and lets the pants fall to the floor, kicking them away. They land on the bed. He throws all the clothes back into the box and closes the lid. He hates the smell of mothballs and aftershave. It clings to his body. He rushes out of the room and slams the door.

Hunter shrugs into trackpants and a t-shirt. He wonders if his mum ever goes into the room and opens the boxes. Why doesn't she burn them? She can't still be hoping he'll return, not after the postcard he sent her last week.

New Zealand.

Hunter remembers his dad going there twice a year on business. He'd send postcards of sparkling harbours and daredevils bungee jumping and he'd promise that next time, the whole family would go. Hunter wanted to ski, to experience the thrill of sliding down a mountain. He imagines it must be the greatest feeling, even if you have to dress like an Eskimo.

Hunter walks into his mother's room and goes to the second drawer of her dresser. He opens it and pulls out a woollen jumper. Underneath is a photo of the three of them at a coffee shop. Hunter is sitting in the middle. On the table near him is a thickshake in a tall glass, topped with chocolate ice-cream. To the left is his mother, smiling at the camera. To the right, his father, looking past the photographer, across the street. His eyes are hooded and he's leaning forward, like always.

The front door slams and his mother calls his name.

Hunter puts the photo back and covers it with the jumper.

11

jesse

Dinner tonight is free-range roast chicken with gravy, potatoes and beans. Dad comes to the table wearing an eye patch. Beth groans. 'What are you, a pirate?'

'Beth, show a bit of sympathy,' says Mum. She reaches across and pats Dad's wrist. 'I think he looks quite dashing.'

'Like Johnny Depp?' Dad suggests.

Beth almost pours the gravy on her lap she's laughing so much. It's hard not to join in. Dad is tall, skinny, with a shock of blond curly hair and big ears. He looks as much like a movie star as I do.

'Being a farmer can be quite difficult at times,' Dad explains.

'A farmer!' says Beth. 'Six fruit trees, a watermelon patch and two garden beds doesn't—'

'Doesn't mean we're not making a contribution to saving the planet, Beth,' Mum interrupts.

'Yeah. Imagine if everyone grew their own vegetables,' says Dad.

'There'd be more food for the starving in Africa,' I say, nervously.

Mum and Dad nod in appreciation. I pretend to be very interested in pouring myself a glass of iced water.

'Jesse's right,' says Dad. 'Each of us, in our small way, is helping.'

'How is growing peaches helping the starving Somalis?' asks Beth.

'Ethiopians,' I correct her.

'Ethiopians, Somalis, Burundians, they're all starving,' says Beth, 'and none of them are eating Dad's peaches.'

Mum sighs. 'Beth.'

'Mum.'

'Beth.'

This could go on all night. 'An eight-year-old boy in Ethiopia has never seen a peach, I reckon. He'd think it was a,' everyone is staring at me, 'a mini football or—'

Beth scoffs.

'It's true,' I say, thinking of my friend, Kelifa. His favourite sport is football and he wants to be a professional player when he grows up. If he grows up. He probably wouldn't actually kick a peach around.

He'd eat it. Somebody should warn him about the hard pip in the middle. And to be careful about getting sprayed in the eye with peach juice.

As if on cue, Dad removes his eye patch. 'This thing is irritating me.' He laughs. 'What's a bit of peach juice,' he looks at me, 'compared to the starving in Africa.'

I can't help myself, 'We should try to help the Ethiopians.'

'Yeah, let's send them Dad's peaches,' says Beth.

'Beth,' says Mum.

'I know my own name, Mum, you don't have to keep repeating it.'

'Maybe the school could take up a collection, Beth. You could suggest it to Larry tomorrow?' says Dad.

'He only wants to save the environment, not starving African kids,' says Beth.

'Bet—' Mum stops herself just in time.

'We could donate money,' I suggest.

'Only yesterday, I gave two dollars to a lady in the street collecting for the Salvos,' says Dad. He picks up a drumstick and takes a bite.

'Will she pass it on to the Ethiopians?' asks Beth.

Dad looks hurt.

'Every little bit helps, Beth,' Mum counters.

'We could sponsor a child?' I suggest.

Dad glances quickly at Mum. Maybe they've already been thinking about it. I have to try, for Kelifa.

'For twenty-seven dollars a month, we could sponsor a boy in Ethiopia. Maybe someone who doesn't even have a mum.' Mum looks at me. I continue, 'Or a dad. Someone who's stuck in a small hut with lots of sisters and only a bag of rice.'

'Yes, well. That's a good idea, Jesse,' says Dad, hesitantly. 'Maybe not this month though. What with school fees and—' He notices he's still holding the chicken drumstick and places it back on the plate.

'Forget your peaches, Dad,' says Beth. 'Just send cash.'

I wonder if Kelifa has a picture of Trevor on his wall.

'We could just donate once,' I suggest.

Dad brightens. 'Yeah! Fifty dollars!'

Beth grins. 'That's not much for a pirate. What about all your buried treasure?'

'Two hundred dollars!' says Dad. He looks quickly toward Mum, who appears to have swallowed some chicken the wrong way.

'One hundred dollars?' asks Dad.

Mum nods.

One hundred dollars! Kelifa could buy enough food for three months and have spare change for a football. To practise, for when he becomes an Ethiopian super-star player. All because of me and Dad!

'I know just who to donate to,' I say without thinking.

The table goes quiet.

'You do?' asks Mum.

'I mean … I could do it for you … On the internet, if you want?'

Beth laughs. 'There you go, Dad. Give Jesse your credit card and it's all taken care of.'

'I'd only spend—'

Dad reaches for his knife and fork. 'I'll handle the financial—' He looks at Mum. 'Your mother will handle the financial transactions, Jesse.'

I can picture Kelifa with a football. Tomorrow, I'm going to write a letter to him. Maybe I'll be able to find his address somewhere on the website. I'll tell him about Dad and Mum and our fruit trees and how one hundred dollars is only the start. I won't mention Beth. He'd probably be jealous of me for having only one sister.

12
HUNTER

Hunter walks into the bathroom and takes the scissors from the cabinet under the sink. He stands in front of the bathroom mirror, staring at his hair. He grips the scissors, considering what to do.

Short on top? Yep.

Long at the sides? Too girly.

Straggly bits at the back? Mullethead! No-one at school would have the guts to call him that.

He puts the scissors down on the sink and turns on the cold tap, filling the basin with water. He ducks his head down and scoops water over his hair. The water runs down his back and makes him shiver. He looks again in the mirror. Wet streaks of hair stick to his face, like a gargoyle.

He grins. Now that's a hairstyle. But he can't go to Walter every five minutes to wet his head in order to maintain the look. Not even Sarah would allow that.

He opens the bathroom cabinet, reaches for a fine-tooth comb and runs it slowly through his hair. He picks up the scissors again and starts cutting: a snip here and there, even to uneven, long to short, wet to dry. What does it matter? His hair drops into the basin, floating on the surface of the water. After a few minutes of careful snipping, he looks again in the mirror. One side of his fringe is longer than the other and a strand of hair tips over his right ear while his left ear sticks out, like a clown.

'Uuuummm,' he says. He snips away the long fringe and considers the options. 'Too clunky on top.'

And there's still the back to do. He opens the cupboard beside the bathtub and picks up his dad's old shaving mirror. Holding it behind his head, he can see what the haircut looks like in the bathroom mirror.

In one word?

'Gross.'

He sighs. What now?

He remembers the time a few years ago when he was beginning swimming lessons and he'd somehow paddled into the deep end, away from his group. When he put his feet down to touch the bottom, there was nothing but water. Water and rising panic. He kicked and flapped his arms against the surface of the water, wondering why he couldn't scream. He went under, gulping water before resurfacing and spitting it out. He wanted to yell, but still no voice would come. He flapped and grabbed at vacant air and felt the water filling his ears and nose. Why couldn't he shout?

He reached one arm high into the air as the rest of his body went under. And that's when his mother dived into the pool. She reached him with a few strokes. With her arms circling him, he felt weightless. His breathing settled immediately as she kicked and floated, with him in her arms, to safety. He could smell her perfume mixing with the chlorine. At the side of the pool he gripped the bar and noticed his mum was wearing a dress, soaked and clinging to her body. The water streaked her make-up. Her dark hair shone in the sunlight.

'Are you okay, dear?' she asked.

Hunter nodded. He stretched his legs and stood up in the pool. His mother touched his cheek with her long fingers. They stood in the pool, looking at each other and the din of splashing and laughing children faded away. After a few moments, they both walked slowly through the water to the steps at the shallow end and got out of the pool. His mother's dress dripped as they walked back to his towel. Hunter noticed she was shivering, even though it was a warm afternoon.

The next time they visited the pool, his mother arranged for a different instructor. A gruff old woman who tolerated no nonsense and never took her eyes off her students. Hunter's mum came to every lesson. She wore the same dress, every week. A private joke, between Hunter and her.

He stares once more at his hairstyle reflected in his dad's mirror. He hates it. He picks up the scissors and starts snipping, not caring where he cuts, just taking off as much hair as he can. He's back in the pool, and every snip is one more paddle, one more stroke to safety. Or further into the deep end? Hunter reaches to the back of his head and snips blindly. He feels the tickle of hair against his neck as it falls to the floor. He keeps cutting until his fingers can no longer grip the locks of hair on the back of his head, until there's nothing but awkward stubble. He grabs at tufts of hair around his ears and cuts wildly. He doesn't stop until there are no more locks to cut.

Hunter notices he's breathing heavily, like that day in the pool, short sharp gasps that aren't enough to fill his lungs. He drops the scissors on the floor and looks into the mirror. A grinning bowling ball stares back.

'Ha!'

13

jesse

'It's okay, Trevor,' I whisper. 'It's for a good cause. Kelifa needs the money more than us. And I've also emailed the Japanese Embassy, about Kate's whales.'

Trevor is silent, although the clouds behind him appear to be getting darker. It's night outside my window.

'Can't we just turn the other cheek?' I plead.

Trevor frowns. I must have the wrong psalm.

'You went around helping people,' I reason. 'Why can't I?' I blush. 'Not that I'm comparing myself to you. You're … you're the inspiration. But I won't tell Dad about that. He's a little funny about false gods.'

There's a sound of shuffling outside my room. I put my finger to my lips to alert Trevor. I creep to the door. The shuffling stops. I peer through the keyhole and see an eye staring back at me!

Someone screams!

I jump and stumble across the floor in surprise.

'What the?' says a voice.

I scramble back to the door and turn the knob.

Beth and I stare at each other.

'What do you think you're doing?' she demands.

'Me? I was looking through my keyhole and saw something blobby and gruesome!'

'That was my eye!' she says.

'Well, I wasn't expecting it to be in my keyhole.'

'It wasn't *in* anything,' she pauses, 'except in my face where it belongs.'

'Why were you spying on me?' I ask.

Beth smirks. 'I heard voices. I thought maybe you had someone in your room.'

'Who? Ryan Blake?' I ask.

Beth blushes. 'He's never been in my room. And if you tell Mum, I'll deny it! So was it your imaginary friend again, Jesse?'

We both look toward Trevor. His eyes are downcast, as if to say, don't involve me. I decide I could use a real friend for a change. Even if it's my sister.

'Beth, can you keep a secret?'

We sit together on the edge of my bed.

'Sure. It was weeks before I told anyone Jade was going out with Nathan.' She pats my knee. 'Tell Aunty Beth everything.' She frowns. 'Have you been bedwetting?' She realises where she's sitting and jumps up.

'Beth! I'm too old for that.'

She sits back down, nervously.

Trevor looks down over Beth's shoulder.

'I stole … I borrowed Dad's credit card,' I confess.

Beth's eyes widen. 'Whoa, that's much heavier than wetting the bed.' She frowns. 'You don't still have it, do you?'

'No, I put it straight back,' I say.

'After what?' she asks, one eyebrow raised.

I squirm underneath the gaze of my twin confessors.

'After giving some money to Kelifa.'

'Who the hell is Kelifa?' Beth's voice is dangerously loud. Dad might not have heard, but Trevor did and I don't think he liked the cursing.

I whisper, 'He's an Ethiopian friend.'

'At school?'

'No, on the internet.'

She clutches my hand and squeezes. 'Please tell me you didn't fall for a Nigerian bank scam? They'll max Dad's credit card in a second!'

She stands ready to blab everything to Dad.

I try to drag her back.

'Do I look that stupid?' I ask.

She moves further to the door.

'Beth! It was CARE Australia,' I say.

She relaxes and comes back to the side of the bed.

'Are you sure?'

'Positive. There was a picture of Kelifa standing in front of his hut. It was smaller than your bedroom.' I wonder whether I should tell her about his four sisters. 'And he doesn't have a mum.'

'How much?' she asks.

'Pardon?'

'How much did you give?' Her eyes narrow. Trevor looks down.

'Fifty dollars,' I whisper.

Beth whistles.

I squirm.

'So this is what you were getting at over dinner.'

'I wasn't *getting at* anything. It just came up.'

She grins. 'And Dad promised one hundred dollars.' She whistles again.

'Could you stop whistling please, Beth.'

She sees the anguish on my face. We're both quiet for a long time.

My voice wavers, 'I'm going to tell Dad tonight.'

Beth looks toward Trevor. 'Did he talk you into it?'

'It's not Trevor's fault.'

Beth giggles. 'Calling the picture Trevor doesn't make him any more real.'

Trevor and I pretend not to hear.

Beth stands. 'Come on then.' She reaches for my hand. 'I'll come with you.'

'You will?'

'Yeah, we'll say ... We'll say we were fooling around on the CARE Australia site and I ...' She frowns.

I click my fingers. 'And I just put some numbers into the credit card box and they turned out to be Dad's.'

'Jesse that is the stupidest idea you've had since stealing Dad's credit card in the first place.' We walk down the hallway. 'I'll think of something,' she rolls her eyes, 'something more believable.'

14

jesse

Dad swears, loudly. The noise of something being thrown comes from behind the door. I break out in a sweat. Even Beth looks a little pale.

'Are you wearing make-up?' I ask.

Beth looks at me strangely. 'No, why?'

'No reason,' I say. The pale face is real. It's not fair to make her go through this torture with me, especially if Dad is already throwing things before we've even entered his workshop.

'Psst,' I whisper.

Beth leads me away from the door. 'What now?'

'Sis, I'll tell Dad alone.'

Dad swears again. Beth tries to smile. 'Nah. It'll be okay.' She gulps, 'I can't—'

I hold up my hand and interrupt her. 'Really, Beth. I've got to do it alone.' I try to stand a little straighter.

'Are you sure?' Beth asks.

'I'll just tell the truth.'

Beth grins. 'Did Trevor tell you to say that?'

'Trevor doesn't actually speak,' I reply.

Beth looks to the door. 'Do you want me to wait outside, just in case?'

I shake my head.

'Just think of the starving millions, Jesse,' she says, before creeping quietly up the back stairs and waving from the landing.

A noise like a dentist's drill comes from behind the door. It stops for a second, followed by shuffling and then the drill starts up once more. I knock. The drill keeps going. It seems to be getting louder.

I knock a little harder.

'Who is it?' Dad's voice sounds frustrated.

I open the door and poke my head around. Dad is sitting in the centre of the room behind a sewing machine.

'Hi, Dad.'

'Hi, come in, Jesse.' He holds up my blue jeans. His overalls are in a pile on the floor. 'I'm stitching our old clothes.' He coughs, embarrassed. 'Your mother suggested we make some savings, after our,' he looks at me, meaningfully, 'recent expenditures.'

'Have you already donated, Dad?'

'No, not yet. Tomorrow night. Your mum suggested we do it together, as a family, before dinner.'

He looks quickly toward the door. 'Just between you and me, Jesse, I may have been a bit rash promising one hundred dollars.'

'That's okay, Dad. I understand.' A vision of Kelifa flashes in my mind, his disappointment is easy to imagine. 'Maybe we could pay it in …' I can't think of the word.

'Instalments?' Dad suggests.

'Yeah, like fifty dollars over two months.'

Dad smiles. 'Don't worry about it, Jesse. My credit card can take it.' He stares at the back wall and his eyes have that faraway look he gets when he and Mum talk about holidays. 'Beth's right. Growing fruit and vegies is not enough.' Dad looks around his workshop, cluttered with tools and boxes full of cast-off junk and old appliances. He points to an ice-cream maker. 'That was used for one summer if I remember correctly.'

I swallow hard. I don't want Dad to feel bad because of something I started.

'Dad, I stole something,' I blurt out.

Dad looks surprised. 'You what?'

'I did it for a good reason, but,' my cheeks feel as if they're on fire, 'but I know it's still stealing. I'm really sorry.'

'What did you steal, Jesse?'

'Your credit card,' I say, in a small voice.

'My what!' Dad's hand instinctively goes to his back pocket.

'For CARE Australia ... and Kelifa ... the Ethi-opians,' I blather.

'Who? Where?' Dad looks confused.

'You can get Mum, if you like. I'm sorry,' I say.

Dad stands up from the sewing machine and walks toward me. He takes my hand and leads me over to the old couch in the corner. We both sit down. 'Okay, son,' he says, 'tell me what you did. Slowly.'

I take a deep breath and tell him everything. Well, almost everything. I leave Trevor out of the story. I figure Dad would blame him, even though it's all my fault. Dad listens patiently, although he sighs a little too frequently to make me feel comfortable.

After I've finished my confession, I know Dad is thinking because he's not talking.

'Maybe I could pay it back,' I suggest. 'By working extra in the garden, or,' I gulp, 'you could take it out of my pocket money.'

Dad smiles. 'I stole ten dollars from my dad once,' he says. 'When he found out, I suggested paying it back out of my pocket money too.' He pats my knee. 'Your grandpa charged me interest, to teach me a lesson.'

'You can do that too, Dad, if you want.'

'I'm not a banker, Jesse. No, we'll work this out ourselves.' He looks at me. 'Let me get this straight. You donated fifty dollars to CARE Australia using my credit card.'

I nod. 'I'm going to write a letter to Kelifa to apologise for not being able to sponsor him. But fifty dollars should help.'

'Not to mention the other money,' adds Dad.

I don't know why, but my lip starts to quiver and without meaning to, or wanting to, I start crying. I'm so embarrassed I hide my face in Dad's chest, sobbing. Dad wraps his arms around me and says my name.

We stay like this for a few minutes before I feel strong enough to show my face again. Dad smiles. 'It's okay, son. I cried after telling my dad too.'

'Really?'

'Well, yes, but that's because Grandpa hit me around the legs with his strap a few times.' Dad's voice deepens, as he imitates Grandpa. 'To teach me a lesson. As if the interest charge wasn't bad enough.' Dad's face is serious. 'Things were different when I was young, Jesse. Grandpa was a good dad, just a little old-fashioned.'

I reach across and hug Dad to let him know he's a good dad too.

'And now comes the hard part. Telling your mum,' Dad says.

'Dad?'

'Yeah?'

'We haven't decided on a punishment.'

'Yes, I've been thinking about that, and maybe Grandpa was right.'

I gulp, thinking Dad's suggesting a few straps across the back of the legs. Dad sees me cringing and adds, quickly, 'No, not that!' He laughs. 'It wasn't the strap that made me cry. It was knowing I'd done something wrong.' He looks at me keenly. 'And I suspect you've learned your lesson, Jesse. That awful feeling in your stomach, that's punishment enough.' He stands up. 'Don't do it again. Okay? Stealing is …'

'Wrong?' I suggest.

He nods.

I hug him tightly once more and leave.

Beth is sitting on the back step. 'Not too painful?'

I shake my head, scared I might start blubbering again if I try to speak.

Beth's phone beeps when I walk past her.

She reads the text and smiles.

'Ryan?' I ask.

'He's helping me with homework,' she says.

The drill-like sound starts again in Dad's workshop.

Beth asks, 'What's he doing in there?'

'Building a cage,' I say, 'to keep Ryan out!'

We both giggle.

15

HUNTER

Hunter sits in front of the computer in his room and types 'Queenstown' into Google Images. The screen fills with pictures of snow-capped mountains looming over a vibrant blue lake; a cable car full of smiling people waving from the windows; a man standing on a mountain top wearing a backpack, raising his arms in celebration; and apple trees blooming pink and white in a green field.

It looks like a place where people go for holidays, where only rich people live. Everyone seems happy. But there are no children. His dad will enjoy that.

He closes Google and looks out of his own window. The house next door has a light on, above the front door. Mrs Ainsworth walks out onto the verandah and calls for her dog, Charlie. She holds a biscuit in her hand. Charlie bounds up the stairs, his tail wagging.

Hunter gets up from his chair and flops onto his bed, closing his eyes. He remembers the last time he saw his dad. It was a Sunday, four months ago.

All morning, he'd been excited, wondering what they'd do. He checked the times of the football games at both stadiums, wondering which one his dad would choose. He googled the weather and decided to pack a towel and swimmers, just in case. Maybe his dad would buy him a boogie board? He jumped up as soon as he heard the car horn. Mum tried to convince him to take a jacket. Hunter had laughed, he didn't need a jacket at the beach. He raced down the driveway and jumped the fence in one casual bound. He hopped in the car. His dad said hello and sped off up the street, before Hunter had even fastened his seatbelt. The conversation went like this:

'How are you, Hunts?'

'Good,' Hunter placed his bag on the floor under his seat.

Mr Riley shifted gear, elaborately, and turned onto Benson Freeway. Hunter wondered what that distinctive smell was. He looked around the interior of the car at the leather seats and the wood-grain dashboard. He turned and looked behind. Nothing but an old frisbee on the rear seat. The car rumbled along the double-lane freeway. Hunter felt like he was sitting in a massage chair. He wondered if they were heading east, to the beach.

'I'm thinking of adding a racing stripe,' Mr Riley said.

'What?'

'A racing stripe, black and white, like the '67 Mustang.' He smiled. 'Didn't you notice my new car? I had a Matchbox model just like this when I was your age. You like cars, don't you, Hunts?'

'Hunter,' he corrected his father. You shouldn't have to tell your dad your name, he thought.

'Come on, I've always called you Hunts,' his dad said.

Hunter shrugged. They drove on in silence. Hunter kept stealing glances at his father. He wondered why he smiled all the time. Why he leaned forward, even when driving, his hands holding the steering wheel loosely, eyes narrowed, squinting into the sun. His sunglasses dangled from the rear-view mirror, swaying back and forth every time they rounded a corner. It began to irritate Hunter. He'd rather his father hid behind the glasses.

His hair was different from last time. It was longer and swept back off his forehead, lacquered around his ears and curled up at his shirt collar. Hunter stared. He was wearing gel. At his age. That was the smell in the car: hair gel, aftershave and leather.

As if reading Hunter's mind, Mr Riley wound down the window.

'It's a good day for swimming, Dad,' Hunter said.

His dad swept a hand over his hair and wound the window up, checking his appearance in the mirror.

'Hunts, I've got a surprise for you,' Mr Riley turned to Hunter, grinning.

'Yeah,' Hunter replied, picturing a boogie board in the car boot.

'In the back seat, Hunts.'

Hunter looked around again. All he could see was the green frisbee. He looked at his dad.

'There's a park near my place on the harbour. We can throw it.'

'I know what to do with a frisbee,' Hunter said.

His dad slammed on the brakes. A car in front had stopped to let a woman and two children cross at the zebra crossing. Mr Riley swore under his breath then checked his watch. Hunter wondered how long they could throw a frisbee.

He reached across Hunter to the glove box and flicked it open. Mr Riley pushed the road atlas aside and picked up a roll of mints, offering one to Hunter. Hunter shook his head. His dad flicked one mint from the packet and caught it in his mouth, looking at Hunter to see if he'd witnessed it. A car horn sounded behind them. The zebra crossing was free. Hunter's dad changed into gear and raced away.

They drove in silence to the park. The harbour water sparkled. Hunter's dad leaned across and pointed to a row of apartments. 'That's where I'm staying,' he said. 'The top one on the left.' Hunter looked up and saw the double doors open to catch the harbour breeze. On the balcony was an exercise machine and … a boogie board.

His dad drove slowly along the street, looking for a car park.

'There's one, Dad,' said Hunter pointing to a shady spot, under a huge tree.

'No way, Hunts,' he said. 'Those trees drop things onto my car. We have to park out in the open.' They drove around in the heat for a few more minutes, before finding a spot.

'Let's play frisbee, Hunts,' said his dad, bounding out of the car.

Hunter wondered whether he should bring his bag with the towel and swimmers. The harbour was almost as good as the beach.

Mr Riley was already standing on the high ground near the poplar trees along the foreshore, waving his arms. 'You go over there, Hunts,' he yelled, pointing near the water's edge. Hunter ran to the spot. Just below him were a young couple in swimmers, sharing a towel on the white sand, their child playing in the shallows picking up handfuls of water and throwing it into the sky. The child giggled when the shower landed on his upturned face. The frisbee zipped over-head and landed a few metres behind Hunter. His father yelled, 'Almost got you!'

Hunter, already sweating, walked to pick up the frisbee. He held it in his hand and noticed the name 'Nathan' printed on the rim in black texta. He covered the name with his hand and looked to where his father stood. He flung the frisbee with all his might. At electric speed, it flew a metre from the ground, aiming straight for his father. Mr Riley stood and watched it shoot toward him, his hands on his hips. At the last moment, he flung out an arm and caught it effortlessly, pirouetting as he did and flinging it straight back.

For what seemed like hours, his dad insisted on throwing the frisbee. Hunter began to aim the frisbee away from his father, making him run, hoping he'd tire and suggest a swim. But Mr Riley returned the frisbee with childish abandon while more sunbathers strolled down to the sand where they read magazines or listened to iPods or swam in the cool water. Hunter wished he could do the same.

Finally, Mr Riley whistled and waved for Hunter. At last, Hunter thought. But when he joined him, his dad grinned and said, 'Try this, Hunts.'

Mr Riley gripped the frisbee and turned to face the harbour. He checked to see his son was watching and then flung the frisbee high into the air. The frisbee flew out over the water and just when Hunter thought it would drop, it turned like a boomerang and sailed unerringly back to where they were standing. His father picked it up, laughing. 'How's that?' he called to no-one in particular.

'Can I have a go?' Hunter asked.

His dad looked at the frisbee in his hands. 'Sure, Hunts,' he said, reluctantly, 'but let me show you once more how to do it.' He walked closer to Hunter and held out the frisbee. 'You have to aim higher and when you release it, flick your wrist. That way it'll bend and return.' He grinned. 'It's a real skill.'

His dad threw it again and, sure enough, the disc shot out over the water and returned, this time with even more backspin and force. It zipped over their heads and landed near a group of senior citizens sharing a thermos of tea on a park bench. Mr Riley ran to pick it up. He ignored the old people.

'You reckon you can do it, Hunts?'

'Sure,' Hunter said.

Hunter sits up in bed and laughs, quietly, so as to not disturb his mum. He recalls the look on his father's face when the frisbee shot out over the water and kept going. Hunter had thrown it with every ounce of energy in his body. He guessed it travelled sixty, maybe seventy metres before plunging down into the deep water. No way his father was retrieving that frisbee. It was gone. Bye bye, Nathan.

*

'Oops,' said Hunter. Such a simple word, he thought, with so much meaning.

'Geez, Hunts, that wasn't ...' His father's words fell away, like a leaf tumbling in the wind. They both looked out across the water. A ferry approached from the west, on a collision course with the green plastic disc. Hunter could see the captain standing alone at the wheel and below him on deck were tourists in sunhats, filming the idyllic beach, the swaying line of poplar trees and the father and son in the park, gawking. They watched the ferry run over the frisbee. Hunter saw it bob, valiantly, on top of the approaching wave for a second, before disappearing under water. Broken to pieces, Hunter hoped.

Hunter looked around. His father was sitting on a bench seat under a poplar. Hunter hadn't noticed him move. He watched the ferry recede into the distance, among the sails of bobbing yachts and hovering sea-gulls. On the opposite headland, a man held a kite in his hands, while a boy stood with the kite line a few metres away. The child ran and the man released the kite. It rippled into the sky, floating higher as the boy ran. The man kept his arms raised, as if in worship. Finally, Hunter walked to the seat and sat beside his father.

'I'm moving to New Zealand, Hunts,' his father said. 'I've arranged for a ship to transport my car.'

Hunter wondered how much line was left on the kite. Just how high could it float?

'I've been offered a job. And,' he looked at his son, 'I've met a woman called Patsy.'

'Ha!' Hunter gets up from bed and quietly opens his bedroom door. The light shines from under his mother's door. She's probably reading in bed. He creeps along the hallway and walks downstairs to the kitchen. He doesn't want to think about his father anymore. He doesn't want to hear about New Zealand and the skiing holidays his dad promised that would never arrive. He doesn't want to visit geysers or bubbling hot mud baths. And he certainly doesn't want to hear about anyone named Patsy. Hunter doesn't want another mother.

16

jesse

The next morning, I have trouble choosing what to wear. I throw all the t-shirts from my drawer out on the bed. There are six black shirts and one dark green one. I look up at Trevor. 'Looks like it's black, again, Trev,' I say.

At breakfast, I eat two poached eggs. Mum stands beside the stove watching me. She's been hovering all morning, serving me breakfast, refilling my glass with orange juice as soon as I take a sip, offering me extra toast. When I finish the poached eggs, she scoops the plate up from the table and rinses it under the tap.

'Can I make you another slice of toast, Jesse, with raspberry jam?' she asks.

'Thanks, Mum. But I'm full.' I rub my stomach for effect.

'Are you okay?' she asks.

Maybe I rubbed too dramatically? 'I'm fine,' I say. Actually, I'm a little queasy from eating all the food she's prepared for me. I feel guilty eating so much when Kelifa is still waiting.

'Jesse?' Mum looks concerned.

'I'm fine,' I repeat.

Mum coughs. 'Your father told me,' she looks toward their bedroom, 'about the incident.' She reaches across and pats my arm. 'I've packed a little treat in your lunch box.'

Why is she being so nice? Did Dad make up a story about me doing something good rather than stealing his credit card? She presses my face against her stomach in a big hug. 'I just want you to know how proud—'

Beth walks into the kitchen and sees us hugging. Mum lets go of me and walks back to the benchtop. 'Beth, what do you want for lunch?'

'Ten dollars thanks, Mum,' smiles Beth.

'To eat, Beth?' Mum holds up a block of cheese and a loaf of bread.

'Okay. Five dollars,' Beth says. 'We have a healthy food canteen, remember?'

'And we have a limited budget,' responds Mum. 'Bread and cheese?'

'Five dollars!' implores Beth. 'It's hardly going to break the bank is it?'

'Beth!' Mum says, a wisp of hair falling in front of

her eyes. She whispers, 'Not in front of …' Her eyes flit toward me.

Beth groans. 'Jesse heard that, Mum.'

Mum busily butters a slice of wholemeal bread and pulls open the second drawer, looking for a sharp knife to cut the cheese.

'Don't bother, Mum,' says Beth. 'Ryan will buy me lunch today,' Beth winks at me, 'and then I'll owe him one.'

Mum looks up quickly, her hand clenching the knife. She bites her lip and searches the kitchen until she locates her handbag among the envelopes and unpaid bills on the bench. She reaches for her wallet, takes out some coins and places them on the table. 'Well, it is a good canteen, I suppose. And we should support it.'

Dad walks into the kitchen and opens the fridge, staring absentmindedly inside. Mum finishes making the sandwich, wraps it in wax paper and places it into a brown paper bag, offering it to him. Dad holds it in front of him, a questioning look on his face.

'It's a cheese sandwich, Dad,' Beth says.

Dad shakes his head. 'Nah, Brian and I are going to the Berliner Cafe for lunch,' he says. 'Chicken schnitzel, rosti and mushroom sauce. Now that's a lunch!' Mum gives him a look and makes a clicking sound at the back of her throat.

Dad puts the paper bag in his briefcase, adding, 'But I could have this before going to the cafe,' he looks at Mum, 'and just have a coffee with Brian.'

'We all have to make sacrifices,' says Beth, casting a glance my way, 'now we're on a budget.'

Dad coughs and everyone looks at me.

'What?' I ask.

'Nothing, Jesse,' says Mum. 'Beth, why don't you walk to school with your brother again? Like yesterday.'

'What, are we budgeting petrol as well,' moans Beth.

'Still saving the planet, Beth. Climate change, remember?' Dad reaches toward the hook for the keys to his Subaru.

'You could ride your bike, Dad,' Beth suggests.

Dad smiles. 'I'd love to, but I'm wearing a suit.'

'Fine, let Jesse borrow your bike,' suggests Beth.

'Beth, walk with Jesse,' Mum interrupts, 'or use that money I gave you for a bus fare.' Mum smiles, knowing Beth won't catch a bus.

I get up to leave the table.

'Have a lovely day, Jesse,' Mum says.

'What about me?' asks Beth.

'Yes,' says Mum, putting her wallet back into her handbag.

As we're walking to school, Beth places a sisterly arm around my shoulder. 'So what's your secret, Jesse?'

'Me?'

'The hugs from Mum, the two-course breakfast. I bet you didn't have to beg for five dollars for lunch,' she says.

'Actually, Mum gave me ten dollars,' I say, in a quiet voice.

'What?' Beth removes her arm and stares at me.

'You can have half, if you want,' I say.

'It's not the money. It's how they're treating you and ...' Beth frowns.

'And all I did was steal Dad's credit card,' I finish the sentence for her. I shift my backpack from one shoulder to the other.

'It's spooky, isn't it?' she says.

'Maybe they think I'm developing into a klep ... kleto ... A person who steals things without meaning to,' I say, my hands shaking at the thought of not being able to stop myself from stealing stuff. What's next? Dad's Subaru for joy rides around the suburb? An iPod from the department store? Hunter's backpack? That would mean certain death.

'Jesse. You're not a kleptomaniac,' says Beth.

'How do you know?'

'Because you can't even say the word!' She giggles. 'And you stole for a good reason.'

'Maybe that's why Mum's being nice to me.'

Beth snorts. 'Great. To get into Mum's good books, I shouldn't clean my room or help her stack the dishwasher. To be a good daughter I've got to plunder the family riches.'

'Sis,' I say seriously, 'I don't think it would work a second time.'

'I know.' Beth rolls her eyes. 'I was joking.'

She puts her arm around my shoulder again and we keep walking. Ryan is leaning against the fence outside school, admiring the tattoo on his forearm.

'See ya, klepto,' says Beth, as she strides ahead to Ryan. He holds his forearm out so Beth can't miss the tattoo. It looks like a dragon wrapped around a dagger.

'You did it!' Beth shouts.

'Yep. It's called Warlock Dreaming,' says Ryan.

'Is it real?'

Ryan blushes. 'It'll last for two weeks.'

I give them space to admire the stick-on thinking please, Trevor, don't let Beth get a tattoo. Mum and Dad have enough worries.

17

jesse

All morning in class during quiet reading time, I stare at the same page, going over everything that happened yesterday.

Helping Kelifa made me feel good.

Stealing from Dad made me feel bad.

Helping Watson escape from Hunter made me feel good.

Being scared of Hunter makes me feel bad.

Does doing something good always come at a high price?

'Hunter, what are you doing?' Sarah asks.

'Nothing!' I answer.

Everyone in class looks at me. Did I just answer to the name of Hunter? I slink down in my chair. 'Sorry, Sarah, I thought you meant Jesse,' I mumble.

'Yes, the names do sound very ...' Sarah lets the

sentence hang. 'But I was talking to the *other* Hunter.' Everyone turns toward Hunter who is unknowingly holding his book upside down.

'What are you doing, Hunter?' Sarah repeats.

'I'm not doing nothing,' he says.

'Anything,' corrects Sarah.

'What?' says Hunter.

'You're not doing anything,' says Sarah, in a resigned voice.

'Yes, I am,' Hunter says. 'I'm reading.'

The brave ones giggle. I keep silent. Hunter holds up the book, 'What's this then?'

'It's a book, Hunter,' says Sarah.

Hunter smirks.

'And …' Sarah stops speaking and sighs. She leans across her desk and picks up the book she was reading. 'Five minutes more of reading time, class.' She then elaborately turns her book upside down and pretends to read it.

A curse comes from the corner where Hunter is sitting. No-one dares look. Sarah smiles at him. She closes her book and walks behind her desk to sit down.

I raise my hand.

'Yes,' she pretends to forget my name, 'Jesse, isn't it?'

'Sarah, after reading, can we do writing work?'

Everyone groans, except Sarah and Kate.

'What did you have in mind, Jesse?'

'If he says poetry, I'm going on strike!' calls Hunter.

'*He* has a name, Hunter,' says Sarah.

'Yeah, Bleakboy,' whispers Hunter. A few students behind me titter.

'Pardon?' says Sarah.

Kate raises her hand.

'Why don't we practise writing letters, Sarah?' I suggest.

'Emails you mean,' corrects Skye. 'No-one writes letters anymore, except old people.'

'And losers,' adds Hunter.

'Writing letters it is,' says Sarah. 'Anyone in particular you want to write to, Jesse?'

Kate waves her hand, trying to get Sarah's attention. Sarah ignores her and looks at me.

'I thought we could try writing to the Japanese Embassy, Sarah,' I say. 'About the whales.'

'Not the whales again, Sarah,' pleads Skye.

'To save the whales,' I add. 'A letter, an email to …' I can't think of the word.

'A protest letter!' Kate calls out.

Sarah winces. 'Kate, raise your hand if you wish to speak.'

'I did.' Kate raises her hand a little higher and twinkles her fingers as if to convince Sarah.

Sarah sighs, 'Okay.' She looks at the clock over

the door. 'I'll give you all twenty minutes to write a letter,' she looks at Kate, 'to anyone you wish.'

Kate groans.

Sarah continues, 'But the letter has to try to convince a person, or an organisation, to stop doing something harmful to the planet.'

Kate starts writing before Sarah has finished speaking, her pen flowing across the paper.

Skye raises her hand.

'Yes, Skye?'

'Can I write an email,' she glances at Kate, 'to someone to stop them eating whales?'

'Exactly!' says Kate. She scribbles something on a piece of paper and hands it to Skye. Skye takes it, nervously.

'It's the address of the Japanese Embassy, Skye,' explains Kate.

'I was talking about writing to you,' says Skye.

'I don't eat whales!' Kate looks horrified. 'The Japanese, Canadians and Norwegians do. Well, some of them do.'

'Yesterday, you were talking about eating—'

'It was a protest!' shouts Kate.

'Kate, will you stop shouting,' pleads Sarah. 'We get your point.' Sarah looks at the class. 'Everyone, please just write.'

'I'm going to do a manga comic,' says Eoin. 'The Japanese love manga.'

'They eat comics?' asks Anastasia, confused.

'No, it's like Batman, only with more violence,' adds Eoin.

'We'll leave out the violence for today, Eoin,' says Sarah.

'Sarah, can I use the computer to write my email?' asks Skye.

'Paper first. If you like the letter, you can transfer it later.' Sarah sits at her desk, putting her head in her hands.

Saving the world can be very tiring. And confusing.

After fifteen minutes, I've run out of things to write. I look around the class. Eoin is balancing a pen on his knuckles, his hand extended over his desk, eyes narrowed, concentrating on keeping the pen level. Anastasia is staring at the ceiling, her lips moving in time to a song in her head. She closes her eyes and mimes the words. Skye is looking at her iPhone, hidden under her desk. Sarah is preoccupied drafting her own letter. The only other people still writing are Kate and Hunter.

Hunter?

I turn in my chair to get a better look, but his desk is too far away. He's so involved in what he's doing, he doesn't notice me staring. He sure looks different with his bowling-ball haircut. Kate looks up and I motion toward Hunter. She grins, pleased that even Hunter has got into the spirit of protest.

'Have you finished, Jesse?' Sarah asks.

Eoin drops his pen and it clatters on the floor. Anastasia stops miming and blushes. Skye hides the iPhone in her pocket. I quickly turn around to face the front. 'Just searching for inspiration, Sarah.'

Sarah stands and walks around her desk. Everyone watches except Hunter who is still intently scribbling.

She walks slowly to the window, smiling at Hunter. We all turn to look. He grips the pen tightly, his face close to the paper. He's scribbling so aggressively that he holds the page firmly with his left hand to stop it scrunching and tearing.

'Hunter,' Sarah says, gently.

Hunter looks up. 'Yes, Sarah.'

'I'm sorry to interrupt.'

'That's okay, Sarah. I'm just,' he elaborately writes a few more words, puts his pen on the desk and adds, 'finished!'

'I'm very impressed, Hunter,' says Sarah, beaming. 'Would you like to read it aloud to the class?'

'Sure would!' Hunter stands at his desk. 'Out front, or here?' he asks.

Sarah smiles. 'At your desk is fine.' No-one can believe what we're hearing. Hunter eager to read aloud in class! Hunter waits until the hum of expectation quietens.

He coughs, theatrically. 'I tried to think of the best way to get the Japanese Government to stop killing whales.' He looks up at Sarah. Kate gives me the thumbs up.

'Very good, Hunter. Continue.'

'Dear Japanese Government and all whale eaters.' Hunter looks up again.

Sarah nods encouragingly.

In a loud voice, Hunter continues, 'If you don't stop killing and eating whales, our army is going to invade your country and blow everybody up! We're going to drop bombs on your buildings and maybe even those schools that cook whales in the canteen. We'll get the Americans to invade as well. It'll be your worst nightmare, thousands of Americans running wild, like in gridiron, only with guns.' Hunter pauses, taking a deep breath. 'You won't have to worry—'

'Hunter,' says Sarah.

'—about eating whales then because you'll all be dead.' Hunter's voice gets louder with every word he says. 'And it serves you right for killing such a beautiful big fat animal like a whale. Dear Minister, do you want to be invaded?'

'Hunter, please!' says Sarah, her voice rising.

Hunter continues, intently, 'Do you want to see your country bombed—'

'Stop!' Sarah shouts, her face turning red with

the effort, and the thought of Japan being obliterated across the pages of Hunter's essay.

Hunter looks up. 'But I've got another page to go, Sarah.'

Sarah draws a deep, slow breath. 'I understand, but killing people is—'

'I'm not killing people, Sarah. I'm threatening. It's the only way to save the whales,' says Hunter. He looks around the classroom, for support. Everyone is pale. Skye looks as if she's going to be sick at any moment. I glance at the door, wondering if she'll make it outside. I stand and walk to the window, opening it wide. A fresh breeze blows through the killing fields of our classroom. A little colour returns to Skye's face.

Sarah coughs. 'Thank you, Hunter, for your contribution.' Her eyes flit from student to student and finally settle on Kate, who has raised her hand, again.

'Yes, Kate?' she asks.

'I think threatening people … defeats the idea of …' Kate stammers.

'Yes, thanks, Kate. I don't think Hunter really wanted to—'

'It works every time,' says Hunter. He sits back in his chair, satisfied.

'But it's not what we do in school, is it, Hunter,' Sarah says, not expecting an answer.

'If anyone eats whales at lunchtime, Sarah, just call me,' answers Hunter.

'I don't think anyone in this school will be eating whales. Remember our no-meat policy.' Everyone nods, except Skye, who raises her hand.

'Skye?' Sarah says.

'Is leather meat, Sarah?'

Everyone looks down at their feet to check their shoes. Today, I have black Dunlop Volleys, made of canvas. I lean down low at my desk to peek at Sarah's boots. Black and shiny and ... dance music starts to signal lunchtime.

Sarah lets out a deep breath. 'We'll do maths after lunch.' She looks at me. 'No questions asked.'

18

HUNTER

After school, Hunter sits on the grass under the maple tree in Elkhorn Park. The woman wearing a grey tracksuit and white headband is doing sit-ups, her personal trainer holding her ankles together, as she struggles to lift her torso off the ground. Sweat stains darken her shirt. The trainer says, 'Just five more.'

Hunter leans back against the tree trunk. He wonders what the woman is thinking, whether she's dreaming about a late afternoon tea of sweet apple pie and a coffee, as a treat after all that effort. Or whether she'll struggle home and consume a handful of nuts, determined to lose weight no matter what.

'No bags to throw around today, young man,' says a voice from beside Hunter. It's the old man on the mobility scooter. Hunter checks the man's shopping basket on the handlebars. Only a newspaper today.

'I was helping a friend,' Hunter says.

'Mmm,' says the old man. He looks across at the woman and the personal trainer, 'Do you suppose anyone enjoys all that effort?'

'Yep. The trainer who gets paid for telling her what to do. What a job,' says Hunter.

The old man smiles. 'Do you get told what to do?'

Hunter shrugs, 'Sometimes.' He thinks of his dad and the frisbee. 'Doesn't mean I'll do it though,' Hunter adds.

The old man laughs until he starts coughing. He takes a handkerchief from his trouser pocket and coughs into it again. As he returns the hankie, he says, 'People tell me what to do'.

'But you're an adult,' says Hunter. He can't imagine who'd have the courage to boss this old man around.

The old man scoffs, 'Old people and children. We're not so different.'

The trainer offers his hand to the woman and helps her up. They set off on a jog around the park. The trainer leads, skipping, clapping his hands over his head and star-jumping, exhorting the woman to do the same. The woman follows in stumbling imitation.

'It's always the relatives,' says the old man. 'They think they know better.' He shakes his head, as if trying to clear his mind of the thought. He moves his scooter closer to Hunter and holds out his hand.

'My name's Les.'

Hunter stands and shakes the old man's hand.

'Hunter.'

'Good to meet you, Hunter.' The old man reaches for his pipe and considers lighting it, before putting it back into his pocket. He cracks his knuckles and rests his hands on the handlebars.

'Here's the deal, Hunter. I'll tell you one thing that annoys me,' the old man says, 'and you can do the same. And I mean really let rip. Swear if you want. Just get it off your chest.'

Hunter shrugs, not sure he wants to tell a stranger, even someone who's introduced himself, his thoughts. He says, 'Okay.'

The old man laughs. 'I was hoping you'd say that.' He takes a deep breath. 'I hate it when people in shops, or in the street talk really slowly to me, as if I'm stupid. As if being stuck on this scooter for half the day has somehow slowed my brain.' The old man tugs his right ear. 'I don't mind when they raise their voices,' he continues. 'I'm a bit deaf, so that's okay. I'm feeble of bone, not brain.' The old man cracks his knuckles again. 'Pretty soon, they'll be imitating baby talk to me. I swear the first time that happens,' he clenches his fist in frustration, 'I'll ...' He stops talking, takes a deep breath, removes the pipe from his pocket and lights it. He leans back in his scooter and looks into the distance.

A bus pulls up and two teenage schoolgirls get out. Both are listening to iPods through earplugs. They wave to each other and set off in opposite directions. As one girl walks along the path near Hunter and Les, her phone rings. She answers in a loud voice, her iPod competing with the phone. 'What?' she shouts. She listens intently to the phone, before switching off her iPod and answering. 'He didn't. Really? That is so …' A voice crackles from her phone. Hunter thinks of his own phone in his pocket, wondering if he has any messages from Mum.

Les watches the girl walking away. 'Do you know the word I hate most in the English language?' he says.

Hunter shakes his head.

'I,' pronounces Les. 'IPhone, iPod, iPad, I, I,' his voice rises. 'It's the ugliest word invented.' He leans close as if he's about to tell a secret. 'And *we* is the most beautiful. The sooner society learns *we* instead of *I* …' Les laughs to himself. 'But what am I saying? You were about to tell me the one thing that irritates you, young man.'

Hunter sighs. He'd like to tell the old man about his dad leaving and what he really thinks of school. It would certainly include lots of swearwords.

'One thing that irks you?' says Les.

Hunter jumps up, reaching for his schoolbag.

'I got a hundred things.' He takes a few steps away from the old man and pulls out his phone, holding it up. 'Maybe next time, okay?' He waves and then runs, his bag swinging against his side, almost tripping him as he reaches the path beside the creek. He doesn't stop running until he's out of sight, sure that he's alone.

He takes a deep breath, drops his bag on the path and spits into the creek. He sees a lizard scurry for cover near his feet and closes his eyes.

He remembers his father smiling as he told Hunter about his plans for New Zealand. He remembers the promises his father made, hovering just out of reach, like a spinning frisbee.

19

jesse

'Dinner,' Mum calls down the hallway.

Trevor and I have been having a one-sided debate about whether Hunter's idea of threatening thousands of people in order to save the whales made sense. We agreed it didn't, but neither of us volunteered to point this out to Hunter. Trevor preached that every life is sacred, human or animal. I didn't want to mention the loaves and fishes. Maybe it should have been the loaves and lentils?

I follow Beth into the kitchen. In the centre of the dining table is one candle, casting a feeble light. Dad closes all the curtains as Mum serves the food.

Beth sits down and looks at the small serving of boiled rice on her plate. 'What's this?' she asks.

'Rice, sis,' I say.

'I know that, fool.'

'Beth, don't call Jesse a fool,' says Mum. 'It's your dinner.'

'Is that all?' says Beth.

'No, of course not,' says Mum.

Beth relaxes.

Mum walks to the kitchen bench and picks up a small saucepan, tips the contents into a bowl and brings it to the table. She puts it next to the candle, so we can see what's in the bowl. It looks like four potatoes.

'Potatoes,' says Beth, predictably enough.

'Actually, no,' says Mum. 'They're yams, a staple food in Africa.'

Everyone looks at me.

'In honour of our donation,' says Dad, 'we thought we'd have a typical African meal.'

'Just like …' Mum looks at me.

'Kelifa,' I say.

'This is probably what he's sitting down to right now,' says Mum, cupping her hand over the candle. 'They're huddled around one flickering candle, just like us.'

Beth makes a noise.

'Don't growl at the dinner table, Beth,' says Mum. 'Be grateful for the food.'

A puff of wind blows out the candlelight.

'At least now I don't have to look at what I'm eating,' mumbles Beth.

Dad scrapes back his chair and feels his way to the kitchen. 'Honey, do you know where the matches— OW!'

It sounds like Dad's head is arguing with the cupboard. Mum gets up and turns on the kitchen light. Dad is sitting on the cork floor, rubbing his head. 'I wonder if Kelifa's dad walks into cupboards,' he says.

Mum helps him to his feet and brings a box of matches to the table. She lights the candle again.

'Some people think candlelight is very,' Mum looks lovingly toward Dad, 'romantic.'

Beth growls again.

'Jesse,' Mum says, 'your father and I thought we'd have this special meal tonight because we looked at our budget and …' Mum casts a worried look toward Dad.

'Ha!' says Beth.

'Aren't we going to send Kelifa something?' I plead, fearing the worst.

'He can have my yam,' suggests Beth.

'Remember what we said last night about instalments,' interrupts Dad, still feeling for a lump on his head.

'Yeah,' I say, 'but we're still going to send Kelifa some money?'

'Apart from the fifty dollars already,' says Beth, who is obviously taking her hunger out on me and Kelifa.

'Your mother,' Dad looks toward Mum.

'My hours got reduced at the cafe today, Jesse,' Mum says. 'Now, it's only three days a week, starting Wednesday.'

I look worryingly at Dad. 'What about your job? You haven't been sacked have you?' Dad is the complaints officer at the local council. Maybe someone complained about him!

He attempts a laugh. 'No such luck, Jesse.' He reaches across the table and touches my hand. 'But, I'm afraid it will have to be only fifty dollars this month for your African friend. And maybe another fifty next month, if things start looking up.' He looks at me. 'But, it can't be long term.'

I feel bad making Mum and Dad worry about Kelifa and me. It's not their fault. It's mine. I'm the one who started all this.

'We don't have to send any more money.' I bite my lip, hoping Kelifa and Trevor will forgive me.

'Great,' interrupts Beth. 'I need a new dress for the weekend. Ryan's—'

'No, Jesse,' says Mum. 'We all need to think of others.' She looks at Beth.

'I am thinking of others, Mum. Imagine Ryan having to see me in the same clothes day after day. I was hoping to surprise him,' says Beth.

'The sewing machine is in your father's workshop, Beth. I'd be happy to buy you some dress material,' answers Mum.

Beth rolls her eyes. 'You're kidding, right?'

'I'm sure Kelifa doesn't get new clothes,' says Mum.

'He's a boy in Africa! He's not going to see The Scrambles on the weekend!'

'Who, or what are The Scrambles?' asks Mum.

'They sound like a death-metal band,' says Dad.

'Death what?' asks Mum.

'I saw it on a documentary,' explains Dad. 'They wear black clothes, play distorted guitars and growl.'

'That explains a lot,' says Mum, glancing at Beth.

'The Scrambles sing folk songs, Mum.' Beth looks my way, daring me to contradict her. 'They write about animals and peace and hope and ...' her voice peters out.

'Yeah, they're actually a harmony death-metal band,' I add. No point in Beth suffering any more torment. Not after the strains of tonight's dinner. The yam on my plate looks sad and lonely and not very nourishing. Poor Kelifa, having to eat that every day. I scoop some plain rice onto my fork and take a big mouthful. I hope fifty dollars allows his dad to buy sauce to flavour his rice. A piece of long-grain gets stuck in my teeth. I reach for a glass of water.

'So The Scrambles are a Beth-metal band?' Dad grins.

'Anyway,' says Mum, not really in the mood for jokes, 'we thought we'd have this dinner to better understand the plight of children elsewhere in the world.' She looks at me. 'And Jesse, we'll see about next month's donation. Maybe we can have this dinner once a week. That'll save us some money.'

'Great,' I say, scooping another forkful of rice into my mouth.

'I'm eating at Ryan's next week,' says Beth.

I wonder if Kelifa has friends in the village where he lives: friends he can visit for dinner when he's bored of a scoop of rice and a yam, rich friends who keep chickens and have eggs, friends who can afford electric lights and maybe even a radio. Or a television.

Beth sprinkles extra salt and pepper on her yam before mushing it up with her fork and mixing it with the rice. 'Baby food,' she mumbles.

The candle flickers again, but doesn't go out.

20

Jesse

It's lunchtime at school and I've picked up a burning cigarette from the path.

'Jesse James Jones!'

I swallow quickly, my throat feeling as if it's on fire.

'Jesse! What on earth are you doing with that cigarette?'

I hide it behind my back, but I don't think that's the answer Rachel, the year four teacher, expects.

'Nothing, miss.' Smoke drifts around my head, like a guilty halo.

Rachel steps forward, a look of concern furrowing her brow.

'Jesse, you know we don't address teachers like that at this school.'

'Sorry, Rachel,' I say in a quiet voice, hoping the cigarette has burned out.

'First names only,' Rachel says. She steps closer, holding out her hand. I'm so nervous, I'm not sure if she wants to shake my hand or take my cigarette. Correction, take Hunter's cigarette. I decide to offer the cigarette. My hand is shaking as I hand it over.

'Smoking is very serious, Jesse.'

'And bad for your health,' I add, coughing. Why would anyone be stupid enough to smoke?

'Why were you smoking, Jesse?' Rachel asks, as if reading my mind.

'I wasn't, miss. I mean, Rachel,' I answer.

She raises both eyebrows and holds up the butt.

'I was …' I'm doomed. If I tell her the truth, Hunter will give me an atomic wedgie and toss my backpack under the school bus. If I lie, I'll be given detention for smoking and Larry will send a letter home. That will mean a week of dinner lectures on the evils of smoking from Mum and Dad.

Disco music signals the end of lunchtime. Rachel looks across at the kids all running back to class.

'I won't do it again, Rachel,' I plead.

The sound Rachel makes at the back of her throat is either because she doesn't believe me or she's as overwhelmed by smoke as I am. I check the butt in her fingers. It's extinguished. She doesn't believe me.

'Honest, Rachel,' I say. 'You'd have to be an idiot to want to smoke. It smells like—'

She raises an eyebrow. Have I just admitted to smoking?

'—smoke,' I finish, in a meek voice.

She holds the butt in her hands as if it's dynamite, about to explode at any minute.

'I was about to put it in the rubbish bin, Rachel, when you saw me. I didn't want to start a bushfire,' I explain.

The disco beat fades. We should be in our classrooms now, Rachel standing in front of year four and me in the second row, beside Kate and Skye, in front of Hunter at his desk near the window where he can watch for bushfires caused by him flicking cigarettes at people during lunchtime.

That's the truth I can't tell Rachel.

Hunter was leaning against the gum tree near the path leading up to Panthurst Lookout, blowing smoke rings when I stumbled upon him. I was fetching a tennis ball for a year two kid. This part of the bush is out of bounds but Tessa Biltoff asked me to get the ball for her. I couldn't say no because she was about to cry.

When I threw it back to her, she waved and ran back to the play area, leaving me alone with Hunter.

'Hey, Bleakboy,' Hunter sneered, the cigarette between his fingers, tucked into his palm, to stop the smoke rising.

'Betcha can't blow smoke rings,' he said.

I didn't have an answer for that, so I just stood there.

'You'd be too scared to even have a drag,' he challenged.

I glanced quickly toward the school buildings. No teachers about.

'I dare you,' he said.

'It causes cancer,' I mumbled.

'Your face causes cancer!' Hunter shot back.

'That doesn't make sense,' I answered.

'Your face doesn't make sense,' Hunter said.

This could go on forever.

Hunter took another drag and shaped his mouth to imitate a goldfish blowing smoke rings. As the largest ring floated into the air, he put his hand through it and smirked.

'I'm a genius,' he said.

I should have walked away at that moment.

'Have you ever done anything bad in your life?' Hunter asked.

Apart from stealing Dad's credit card, I once tried to eat Mum's earring, but I was only two years old at the time. Luckily I didn't swallow. And singing along with a rap song when I was six didn't impress Mum. I didn't know the lyrics were all swearwords. And once I pretended to be sick to avoid visiting Aunty Trish, who hugs too tightly and has bad breath.

'You're so good, you're invisible,' added Hunter. He took a final drag of the cigarette and flicked the butt toward me. I jumped out of the way and it landed on the path.

'See ya,' he said, walking away.

The cigarette burned at my feet, smoke drifting upward. I should have stepped on it. Instead, I picked it up and held it close to my nose, sniffing the tobacco. I wiped the butt on my black t-shirt. I didn't want to taste Hunter's spit.

Just one drag.

An experiment.

To see if smoking was as bad as everyone said.

I gingerly lifted the butt toward my mouth, closing my eyes to concentrate.

No!

I couldn't do it. Not because it was wrong, or bad for me. But because the thought of Hunter's spit was too much to bear. I opened my eyes and looked straight at Rachel calling out my name.

I trudge home from school, relieved that Rachel didn't write a letter to my parents. I got two lunch detentions and a stern warning. All afternoon I imagined what Mum and Dad would say if they found out. First stealing the credit card, now smoking. Trying to be good was certainly turning out bad. Even Trevor couldn't solve this latest problem. He'd stare down from the wall at me, disappointed.

'I've got it,' calls Kate, running to catch up.

'Huh?' I mumble. Normally I'd say pardon. Even my manners are turning against me.

'We'll picket the embassy!' she announces.

It sounds illegal.

Kate skips beside me. 'I saw it on the news once. Hundreds of people stood outside this building, holding banners and shouting.' She holds up both hands as if she's carrying a banner and shouts, 'Save the whales NOW!'

An old lady walking her dog ahead of us turns in fright. She grips her handbag. The dog wags its tail. I try to look as friendly as possible. The dog growls. Maybe it's one of those police dogs that can spot a criminal at ten paces.

'It'll be fun,' says Kate. 'Sarah can call it a school excursion. We can make the banners in art class.'

Our school has some unusual ideas, but I can't see them accepting a day of criminal activity as an alternative to maths and geography.

'And what happens after we shout for a few hours?' I ask.

Kate looks uncertain. 'I don't know. The Japanese stop whaling, I guess.' Kate brightens. 'I'll do some reading about it tonight. And tomorrow we'll ask Sarah.'

'We?'

'Come on, Jesse. You're the only one I can trust,' she pleads. She grabs my hand and squeezes. We glance at our hands clasped together, then quickly let go. We both blush and look away. I concentrate on smiling at the old lady. Her dog barks as we overtake them.

'Boris!' she calls. 'They're just schoolchildren.'

Not according to Boris. He knows what we're planning.

'Kate,' I say, 'if I help you with the whales, will you ...'

Kate looks at me, questioningly.

I swallow hard. 'Will you help me with a ...' How can I explain about Kelifa and my parents' financial troubles?

Kate says, 'Don't worry about Hunter, Jesse. Everyone is scared of him. Remember our non-violent protest.' She giggles then stands still, her eyes glazing over as if ignoring Hunter's latest insult.

'It's not Hunter. It's a friend,' I say.

'Which friend?' She blushes again. 'A girl?'

'No, no, no,' I say, a little too loudly. 'A boy I know on the internet.'

Kate shakes her head. 'My dad told me not to chat to strangers on the web.'

'He's not a stranger, he's a boy. And I don't chat to him. He can't afford a computer. I ... My parents sent him a donation. For charity.'

'I could give you five dollars and ask Mum and Dad for a donation. Maybe we could take up a collection from our neighbours?'

'That's it!' I say. 'We can start a fund to help Kelifa!'

Everyone can join in. I'm so excited I give Kate a big hug.

'I knew you'd have an answer,' I say.

She giggles. Our faces are so close, I can feel her breath on my cheek. It smells of spearmint chewing gum. We look at each other, then jump away as if electrocuted. Except Kate's hair isn't standing on end, it's soft and curly and looks bouncy, like in those television commercials for shampoo. I'm not sure who is the most surprised. Me, Kate or the old lady who's caught up to us on the footpath.

'It's not a dance hall, you know,' she says as she leads Boris past us. Boris is wagging his tail at a man walking his German shepherd on the other side of the street. It must be puppy love, I think.

Kate grins, her braces glinting in the late afternoon sun. She notices me looking and closes her mouth.

'I love ... like your braces, Kate,' I say, wondering how long a person can blush before all that blood makes their head explode.

'You're just saying that because I caught you staring,' Kate replies, softly.

'No I'm not. They make ...' I don't know how to explain what I mean.

'Railway tracks, just like Hunter says!' Kate answers.

I feel the blood pumping faster to my face: explosion time five seconds and counting.

'They make you, you!' I say. 'Like my dad has his curly hair. Without it he just wouldn't look right. And Mum has her bracelets and beads and long dresses. And Larry has his t-shirts. We all have something that gives us—'

'And what do you have, Jesse?' Kate smiles.

I shrug, unable to think of a single thing.

Kate reaches for my hand. 'Warm hands. That's what you've got.'

And a face redder than a beetroot.

21
HUNTER

Hunter sits beside the fountain at Elkhorn Park after school. The woman and her personal trainer do circuits of the park, stopping every lap to shadow-box for a few minutes. The trainer calls out, 'Left, right, left,' encouraging the woman. The woman responds with tired punches and exaggerated breathing.

Hunter wonders where the old man is today. He picks up his backpack and walks across the park, following the path beside the creek. His phone beeps with a text message. Mum wants to meet him at Berliner Cafe for a milkshake. Hunter smiles. Anything is better than doing his personal assessment task.

He scrambles down the embankment and hops from rock to rock across the creek before hauling himself up the other side. He wonders if his mum has already ordered a vanilla thickshake with a double scoop of chocolate ice-cream on top. She knows what he likes.

There's a line of bicycles parked outside the cafe. At a table on the verandah, four men sit drinking coffee. They're all dressed in lycra and cycling jerseys. One of them wears a yellow bandana around his head. He looks like an overweight bandit. Hunter tries not to laugh when the waitress brings the man a lemon meringue pie the same colour as his bandana.

Hunter enters through the back door and sees his mum. He decides to surprise her. She stirs her coffee which sits next to a tall thickshake. Hunter smiles. Before he can walk to the table, a middle-aged man wearing a tweed jacket and carrying a single rose approaches his mum.

'Hello, sorry I'm late,' says the man. Hunter hides behind the magazine stand. The man has a jovial round face with pale cheeks and a slightly red nose. His hair is unruly but has been hastily flattened down with water. He smiles easily. 'I missed the bus,' he says.

Hunter's mum looks behind her, as if she thinks the man is talking to someone else.

The man sits down at the table in Hunter's seat and gestures to the waiter for a coffee. The waiter nods and looks at Mrs Riley, questioningly. She shakes her head.

'I'm always missing buses,' the man says. 'A bad habit I've had since I was a child. Of course, being late for school had its advantages.' He laughs. 'It's nice of you to meet me.' He looks around again, toward the waiter. 'I'm not familiar with this part of town. Do you work near here? Is this your local?' He drums his fingers on the table. 'I … I've never done this sort of thing before,' he says. 'I guess that's obvious.'

Hunter feels blood rush to his face when the man offers his mum the rose. At first, Mrs Riley shakes her head as if to say no, but the man insists and she accepts. His mum lifts her hand to her cheek as if to cover her embarrassment. The man says, 'My name's Donald. But, you already know that.'

The waiter brings the coffee and slides it across the table. Donald offers him a five dollar note and says, 'Keep the change'. The waiter smiles and walks away.

Donald notices Hunter's thickshake beside his coffee. He slides the full glass toward Mrs Riley. 'Do you always drink coffee and a thickshake?' he asks.

'It's for my son,' Mrs Riley says, looking out the window.

'Your son?' Donald looks confused. He follows Mrs Riley's gaze. 'Your profile didn't say you had children,' he says.

'My what?'

'Your profile. On Dating Hearts.'

Mrs Riley shakes her head. 'I'm sorry, I don't know what—'

'You're Diane? Aren't you?' Donald blushes.

'My name is Helen.'

He sighs. 'I knew I should have asked for a photo. She said she'd be wearing a blue frock and ...' They both look at Mrs Riley's dress: blue.

'Oh dear,' he says.

Mrs Riley holds the rose in her hand. She lifts it up to her nose and closes her eyes, as if enjoying the delicate perfume. At the noise of a chair scraping back she opens her eyes. Donald is about to stand.

Hunter looks around the cafe for a woman wearing a blue dress. There is no-one but his mum.

The man smiles. 'Please, keep the rose.'

Hunter watches his mum smile at the man. Her eyes twinkle.

'What's Dating Hearts?' she asks.

'A place for,' the man smiles inwardly, 'fools like me, I guess.' He finishes the coffee. 'My wife left me five years ago,' he says. 'It's only now I'm getting up the courage to ...' He places the cup back on the saucer.

His mum holds up the rose again. 'It's a lovely thought,' she says, simply.

'I don't know if I'll have the courage to try again,' he says. Donald looks up and sees Hunter staring at them.

Hunter blushes and steps from behind the stand. He walks to the table. 'Hi, Mum,' he says.

Donald stands and clears his throat. Mrs Riley blushes and puts the rose on the table.

'I'll be going,' he says. 'Thanks for,' he looks at Mrs Riley, 'understanding.' He smiles at Hunter and strides out of the restaurant. Mrs Riley watches him walk past the cyclists.

'I wonder if he'll look back,' she says, in a quiet voice.

Hunter watches his mum look after the man. She's sitting up straight in the chair and biting her lip, as if everything depends upon what the man does next.

Donald turns around and offers a timid wave. Mrs Riley smiles.

Hunter sits down at the table.

'Vanilla thickshake with chocolate ice-cream, dear, your favourite.'

'Who was that, Mum?' Hunter asks.

'He mistook me for somebody else.' Mrs Riley laughs, looking at her son. 'Do I look like a Diane to you, Hunter?' she asks.

Hunter takes a noisy slurp of his thickshake and says, 'You look like my mum, Mum.'

22
Jesse

In class the next day, Kate raises her hand as soon as Sarah walks into the room. Sarah pretends not to notice and shuffles some papers on her desk.

'Good morning,' she says.

'Good morning, Sarah,' we answer. Kate waves her hand to get attention.

'I don't suppose you want to go to Walter, Kate?' Sarah asks.

'No, Sarah,' Kate says. 'Jesse and I have an idea for an excursion.'

Sarah glances at me and I try to look hopeful, without giving too much away.

'Yes?' she asks.

'The Japanese Embassy, Sarah,' announces Kate. I look at Kate's hands. She's crossed her fingers, for luck. I do the same.

'Not this again!' says Skye. 'Can't we go to the beach instead?'

Sarah places the papers in a neat pile on her desk. 'And what would we do at the embassy, Kate?' she asks.

'We'd hold up banners made in art class and ask the Japanese not to kill any more whales,' says Kate, looking around the class for support. Lance stifles a yawn while Anastasia stares out the window.

Hunter raises his hand.

'No, Hunter, we are not going to threaten the Japanese Embassy staff.'

'I didn't say anything, Sarah,' says Hunter, looking hurt. 'I was going to suggest shouting would be better than being polite.' Hunter raises his voice, 'I'm good at SHOUTING, Sarah.'

Sarah winces. 'Yes, I'm aware of that, thank you, Hunter.' She takes a deep breath and looks at Kate. 'I'm sorry, Kate, but I don't think your parents would like me to—'

Kate raises her hand and shakes it around. Sarah nods.

'I've already got a note from my parents saying it's okay,' says Kate, smiling.

Skye raises her hand. 'I haven't, Sarah. My parents would be very upset if I got a criminal record.'

'There's no crime in standing on a footpath, Skye,' answers Sarah.

'And no fun either!' responds Skye.

'I can practise my Japanese language skills,' says Eoin.

Everyone looks at Eoin. Sarah asks, 'And what can you say in Japanese, Eoin?'

'Hello, goodbye, happy birthday,' Eoin bites his lip, thinking, 'and how far is it to Tokyo?'

Sarah smiles.

Anastasia raises her hand. 'Justin Bieber is very popular in Japan,' she says.

'What does that have to do with Kate's idea?' asks Sarah.

Anastasia shrugs. 'We could write to Justin to ask him not to go to Japan until they free the whales.'

'The whales aren't captured,' says Kate. 'They're killed in the ocean.'

'*Tanjoubi omedetou*!' says Eoin, in a loud voice.

'Is that happy birthday in Japanese, Eoin?' asks Sarah.

Eoin nods and looks like he's about to start singing.

I quickly interject, 'We can hand out leaflets letting the public know about the whales getting eaten.'

'Yeah. With lots of pictures of whales cut up and blood and guts hanging out everywhere,' adds Hunter. 'I vote we go to the embassy, Sarah.'

Sarah looks very nervous at the mention of the word vote.

'Good idea, Hunter,' I say. 'Let's have a vote, Sarah.'

Sarah sinks back into her chair.

'I vote for the embassy!' says Hunter. He raises his hand in the air. Everyone follows, except Skye, who crosses her arms and stamps her feet under the desk.

Eoin says, '*Hai*', in a loud voice. We all look at him. He grins, 'It means *yes* in Japanese.'

Sarah sighs.

'Jesse and I will write the leaflet, Sarah,' says Kate.

'I'll look for pictures, Sarah,' adds Hunter.

'I'll write to Justin,' says Anastasia.

Sarah raises her hand. 'Okay. I'll suggest it to Larry.'

Kate grins. Skye groans.

'But we will only hand out leaflets,' Sarah continues, 'without gruesome pictures. Just the facts.'

'The facts are whales get their guts cut open,' says Hunter. 'Why can't we show the truth?'

'We'll tell the truth, not show. That's final.' Sarah looks at Kate. 'Kate, you and Jesse are in charge of gathering all the information we need.' She sighs. 'The rest of the class can design the leaflet and—'

'Practise shouting!' suggests Hunter.

'—workshop a way to approach people in the street that is courteous and friendly,' says Sarah.

Skye raises her hand.

'Yes, Skye.'

'I object.'

'To what? Saving the whales?' interrupts Kate.

'To spending valuable class time standing on a street corner, littering,' says Skye.

'It's not littering,' answers Kate.

'Yes, it is. People throw that stuff on the ground after pretending to read it.'

'I'm happy to make everyone read it, Sarah,' suggests Hunter.

'That's not necessary. We'll hand out the leaflets and hope that's enough. It is a democracy, after all,' says Sarah.

'Not for the whales,' whispers Kate.

'I'll pick up all the leaflets that get tossed away, Sarah. So we can recycle,' I offer.

'Eeeewwww!' says Skye.

'Enough!' says Sarah. 'I'll ask Larry what the school policy is on—'

'Picking rubbish off the ground,' interrupts Skye.

'—on such excursions,' says Sarah.

At lunchtime, I'm sitting under the wattle tree watching the kindy children play hide-and-seek. Paisley Newbould hides behind a pole and closes her eyes. She thinks if she can't see anyone, they can't see her. She's caught immediately by Rain Barker, who dances around Paisley and giggles saying, 'Gotcha, gotcha'. Paisley keeps her eyes shut and ignores Rain. Rain stops dancing and stares at Paisley.

For a minute, all is silent.

Then Rain carefully presses a finger into Paisley's eye and lifts her eyelid.

'Gotcha,' she shouts.

Paisley slaps her hand away. Rain's bottom lip starts to quiver. Paisley yells, 'You poked me!'

'Did not!' says Rain.

'Did too!' shouts Paisley.

I know where this is heading, so I pick up my lunch box and walk away. I should help the kids settle their problem, but the last time I tried to help I ended up on detention for smoking. I walk behind Edith, out of sight of the kindy kids, and sit on the bench seat against the mudbrick wall. Kate sees me and walks across to sit down.

'We did it, Jesse,' she smiles. 'Larry came up to me a minute ago and said the teachers had approved our excursion.'

'No gory pictures,' I say.

'Hunter will be disappointed,' she says. 'Do you want to come over tonight, to help me get the information Sarah wants?'

'Sure,' I say. 'If I'm allowed.'

'It's for a good cause,' says Kate.

'My family has had enough good causes lately,' I say, thinking of Kelifa and our new family budget.

23
HUNTER

'Smoking stinks,' says Hunter.

Les leans back on his scooter, his eyes wide and smiling.

'Don't tell me you tried.' He laughs.

'I couldn't find a pipe,' Hunter says, 'so I borrowed a cigarette from a senior boy.' Hunter stares across the park to the creek, remembering Jesse discovering him. How he tried to make it look cool, worried that Jesse would see him coughing.

'Why would you want to be like me?' Les says. He reaches for his pipe, then thinks better of lighting up, grumbling to himself as he stuffs it back into his pocket.

Hunter leans down for his schoolbag and stands, ready to leave.

'Wait on, young man.' Les grips the handlebars of

his scooter. 'I wanted to apologise,' he says, 'for the other day, trying to get you to say …'

Hunter shrugs. 'It's what adults do.'

The old man smiles. 'You're smarter than you seem, young man.'

'Ha!'

'What?' asks Les.

Hunter looks at his shoelaces, not sure how to express what he's thinking.

'The easiest way is to start at the beginning,' says Les, his voice unusually quiet.

'At school, they think I'm stupid,' Hunter says. 'But today, I managed to arrange that everyone misses out on a whole day of schoolwork.' Hunter laughs, thinking back to how the whole class, except Skye, raised their hand when he led them. A day away from lessons, just hanging out in the city. Too easy.

Hunter and Les watch as the woman and her trainer jog into the park. The woman has a new haircut that bounces as she runs. Hunter notices she's also wearing lipstick. For exercise? She watches the trainer closely and smiles whenever he looks at her. They do a circuit of the park before stopping for a drink at the fountain. The trainer turns on the tap for the woman.

Les steers his scooter closer to Hunter. He holds out his hand. 'Help me out of this thing, will you.'

Hunter steps forward and lets Les grip him by the arm, taking the old man's weight as he pulls himself from the scooter.

'To the bench seat, if you can,' Les says.

Hunter shuffles beside Les. He notices the veins on the old man's hands. Les's breath sounds hollow, like wind whistling through a metal drain. When they get to the seat, Les steadies himself before sitting. 'I should buy a walking stick,' he says.

Hunter sits down beside the old man and waits, wondering why he bothered moving from the padded seat of the scooter. The old man leans away from Hunter and pokes him in the ribs.

'No sitting for you,' Les says, tilting his head toward the scooter.

'What?' asks Hunter.

'Can you ride my scooter?' Les asks. 'I want to see how foolish I look trundling around the suburb.'

Hunter smiles. Secretly, he's wondered how fast the scooter would go. He walks toward the scooter and slides easily behind the seat, resting his feet on the platform. He looks down at the handlebars. A key dangles in the ignition. One turn and he's away.

'The accelerator is on the right handle grip. Twist it toward yourself. The brake is near your right foot.'

Hunter turns the key. The electric motor starts, barely making a noise. He grips the handlebar and feels the hard rubber of the accelerator. Carefully, he rotates his hand and the scooter springs to life, faster than he expected. Hunter grips tighter with his left hand and releases the accelerator with his right. The scooter slows immediately. He looks down at the platform, eyeing the brake. He presses his foot on the pedal and the scooter stops. A tin of dog food rattles in the basket.

'Go on,' calls Les. 'I'll time you. One lap of the park. And no cutting corners.'

Hunter looks at the old man and grins. Les holds up his right arm, looking at his wristwatch. 'On the count of three. One, two ...' Hunter grips the handlebars and leans forward. 'Three!' He pulls quickly on the accelerator and feels himself being pushed back in the seat. He concentrates on steering along the concrete path, on the lookout for mothers with prams and wandering dogs. He releases the accelerator when he reaches the far corner, smiling to himself. It's like riding a bike, only without the effort. The tin of dog food bounces in the basket when he veers off the path to pass a woman power walking.

He can hear the old man laughing from across the grass. Fifty metres to the finish line. He pulls back as far as he can on the accelerator, wishing the machine had a speedo. He leans down behind the handlebars and the grass is a blur beside the path. As he crosses the imaginary line, the old man whoops and Hunter holds up one hand in triumph. He puts his foot on the brake pedal and slows, steering toward Les on the bench seat.

Hunter turns the scooter off and looks at the old man. Both of them are grinning. He reluctantly slides out from the padded seat.

'It's—'

'More fun than you expected,' Les says.

Hunter nods.

The old man grips the edge of the bench seat and pulls himself upright. Hunter reaches toward him. The old man shakes his head. 'No thanks, Hunter. I can make it this far,' says Les as he takes the few steps to the scooter and slowly pulls himself aboard.

'You weren't worried about how you looked,' says Hunter. 'You just wanted to give me a ride, didn't you?'

The old man turns the ignition key and settles back in the seat. He winks.

'Better get the food home for Deefer. Don't want him to starve.'

Hunter sits on the bench seat and watches the old man trundle away. The fingers of his right hand twitch, as if they're still gripping the accelerator.

24

Jesse

Kate and I are sitting on a comfy old lounge on her back deck, watching her dog, Misty, chase its tail. Round and round Misty goes, until she gets so tired she falls in a furry bundle on the grass, whining with dizziness.

Kate has a pen in her hand and an exercise book in her lap. She taps the pen on her knee. 'Come on, Jesse,' she implores. '"Save the whales now!" is a little boring. No-one will read a leaflet like that. We need something catchy.'

'It would help if we could use pictures,' I say.

Kate shakes her head. 'Sarah's Number One Rule: no gore, no,' she giggles, 'rude words.'

I try to imagine what my dad would say. He's the expert in puns.

A whale of a problem.

Worth blubbering about.

All far too embarrassing to say aloud.

Kate sighs. 'We should be able to show the truth. No matter how ugly it is. People like Skye need to understand.'

'Why don't we have a picture of a mother whale and a calf?' I suggest. 'Nothing yucky, just a happy photo of mother and baby. And then a headline like—'

'My baby! Eaten by the Japanese!' says Kate.

'Maybe something less—'

'My baby is not a burger!'

I smile. Kate is already scratching the headline across the top of the page.

'My baby is not a takeaway!' I suggest.

Kate laughs.

She slowly fills the page with writing. She knows everything about the whales and the Japanese without once checking the iPad on the table in front of us. I watch her as she writes. A slight frown line across her forehead gets deeper as she concentrates. She has the lightest freckles on her nose, as if they're fading right before my eyes. Her curly hair is tied in a ponytail with a green ribbon to keep it in place.

'I like green,' I blurt out without thinking.

'Pardon?'

'Green. It's my favourite colour,' I stammer, my eyes straying to the ribbon.

Kate sees me looking and smiles. 'Me too!' She stretches her legs toward the table and rolls up her pants to show me her socks. Green. 'My lucky socks,' she says. Then she blushes and goes back to the whales and Japanese.

'When I rang Dad, I asked him what else we should do,' I say, 'at the protest.'

'And?'

'He said we should form a group with Sarah and ask to see the Japanese Ambassador.'

Kate's eyes sparkle. 'Great idea, Jesse. Me and you and Sarah, and Eoin with his excellent Japanese.'

'Not Hunter.' I giggle, thinking of what Hunter would say. All that swearing wouldn't be very diplomatic.

Kate reaches for a book and offers it to me. 'You can borrow it to learn all you need about whales for our meeting.'

'I don't know if it'll be that easy to get inside,' I say.

'No worries, I'll email the embassy, so they know we're coming.'

'What if they ignore you?'

'Mum says I should contact the newspapers and television stations. She says whenever there's a camera around, people can't say no.'

As if on cue, Kate's mum arrives home from work, carrying a briefcase, her high heels clicking on the timber kitchen floor. She waves to us and mimes having a drink. I'm not sure if she's asking if we'd like a drink, or saying she can't wait to have one herself, so I just smile.

A minute later she carries a tray of soft drinks and chocolate biscuits out to us.

'Hi Jesse.' She smiles. 'Have you and Kate saved the world yet?'

'Almost, Mrs Hughes,' I say.

'Call me Aristea please,' she says.

I wonder what that name means.

Mrs Hughes smiles. 'I bet I know what you're thinking. It means the best ever.' She pours Kate and me a glass of lemon drink. 'When I was Kate's age, I never told anyone that. I used to come up with fake meanings to avoid embarrassment.'

'It's lovely,' I say.

'I've grown into it, you might say.' Mrs Hughes points at the biscuits on the tray. 'Eat them all okay. It'll be hours before dinner.' She walks back into the kitchen, humming.

I reach for a biscuit. 'Aristea, goddess of chocolate biscuits!'

Kate laughs.

I offer her the tray. She shakes her head. 'The chocolate gets caught in my braces.' She blushes.

'That's okay,' I say. 'It means you'll have the taste of chocolate in your mouth for longer.'

Kate reaches for a biscuit. 'You always see the positives, don't you, Jesse?'

My mouth is full of crumbs, so I just nod.

'Maybe we should take a packet of biscuits to the embassy. To encourage them to eat biscuits, not whales,' says Kate.

'Now there's a slogan,' I say.

Kate and I both giggle. Kate says, 'One, two, three,' and together we shout, 'Eat biscuits, not whales!'

Misty whines from the garden and starts chasing her tail again.

25
HUNTER

After school on Friday, Hunter enters the phone number of the Salvation Army into his mobile and listens for a ringing tone. He sits on the bed in the spare room, staring at the boxes of his father's cast-off clothes.

'Hello,' a lady's voice answers.

'Hi,' says Hunter. 'I've got lots of clothes.'

There's silence on the end of the line.

'I don't want them,' Hunter adds. 'They're not mine.' He stands and pushes a box away with his foot.

'You can bring them into the store, if you wish,' the lady says. 'Ask for Margaret.'

Hunter looks at the three boxes in the corner. It's too many to carry.

'Um, okay,' he says. Three trips to the shops just to get rid of a bunch of rags.

'I'll be here until five today,' Margaret says, before hanging up.

Hunter sighs and tosses his phone onto the bed. He lifts the top box in both hands. It doesn't weigh much, but he can't carry all three to the shops in one go. Maybe he should just leave them on the footpath and hope someone will take them away.

He walks into his bedroom and looks out the window. Mrs Betts is wheeling the rubbish bin out to the gutter. He looks down the street. Everyone's bin is on the footpath, like a sentry line of smelly soldiers. Hunter imagines himself under cover of darkness, running up and down either side of the street, dumping his father's clothes into each bin. A shirt here, a jacket there. He giggles. He could set the stopwatch on his phone. How long would it take to remove all traces of his father?

He thinks of all the homeless people who could use the clothes. Kate and Jesse would definitely take them to the Salvos. Maybe he should phone Bleakboy. He's such a do-gooder, he'd come round and help carry the boxes to the shops.

'Ha!'

He walks downstairs to where the rubbish bin stands beside the garden shed. He tilts the bin, opens the side gate and pulls it onto the footpath. He checks his watch. Still an hour until Mum gets home from work. He walks around the back but before going inside, he spies his old skateboard next to the shed.

Hunter picks it up and spins the wheels. A little squeaky, but they still roll. He carries it upstairs to the spare room and puts it on the floor beside the boxes. Carefully, he lifts a carton and balances it on the skateboard. He stacks a second box on top. Then a third. The pile looks cumbersome and awkward. Hunter stands behind the boxes and pushes them across the bedroom floor. The skateboard trundles along.

'Ha!'

Hunter lifts the top box from the pile and carries it downstairs and out to the footpath. He races back upstairs for the next box. Soon enough, Hunter and his dad's clothes are rumbling down the footpath toward the shops. When he gets to the bottom of the street, he slowly turns the wide load and it clatters across the road. A woman in a four-wheel drive smiles as she waits for Hunter to get to the other side.

The gutter looms in front of him. Normally, there's a flat section for cyclists, but not here. Hunter pushes the skateboard into the gutter and unloads one box at a time. He kick-flips the skateboard onto the footpath and reloads the boxes. He's sweating with effort when he reaches the Salvation Army store three doors down from the Berliner Cafe. He remembers his mum and the man at the cafe. His mum smiling as she held the rose.

A woman wearing a black-and-white chequered dress with white stockings comes out of the Salvos and, when she sees Hunter's load, holds the door open for him. He wheels the skateboard through the doorway.

'Men's or women's clothes?' the woman asks.

'My dad's,' Hunter answers.

'Oh well,' the woman says, before walking away.

Hunter hears the bell above the door tinkle as it shuts behind him. He pushes the boxes along the lino floor toward the counter.

A woman wearing glasses with a purple scarf covering her hair walks out from the rear of the store.

'So, what have we here, young man? A year's supply of comics? Broken toys and a video game from the dark ages?'

'Are you Margaret?' Hunter asks.

The lady tilts her glasses and looks at Hunter. 'One and the same,' she says. 'Did you ring earlier about clothes?'

Hunter nods.

'Well, bless me, finally we may have a donation that doesn't go straight to the tip.' She opens the top box and pulls out one of Hunter's dad's work shirts, nodding approvingly. She lifts a few more shirts from the box, holding each one up to the light, inspecting the collars and the stitching along the sides.

'Excellent quality, young man,' she says. 'I won't even bother checking the other two boxes. You have a trustworthy face.'

No-one has ever said that before, Hunter thinks.

'May I ask whose clothes they are?' Margaret says.

'My dad's.'

Margaret removes her glasses.

'And he's?' She bites her lip and waits for Hunter to finish the sentence.

It occurs to Hunter that she thinks his dad is dead.

'He's gone to New Zealand,' Hunter says.

'Oh, I see,' says Margaret. 'Well, you can thank your mum for sending us these.'

Hunter wonders why she's thanking his mum. It was his idea.

'It's very kind,' Margaret adds.

Hunter unloads the boxes and places them near the counter. He picks up his skateboard and walks out of the shop. On the footpath, he looks back and sees Margaret folding and stacking the shirts on the counter.

He drops the skateboard, places a foot on it and skates along the footpath, weaving in and out of pedestrians and cafe tables. He can't help but smile. Almost as much fun as riding Les's scooter.

'Hunter!' a voice calls.

He slows and looks around.

On the verandah of the Berliner Cafe is his mum. She holds up her mobile.

'I was just about to text you for a thickshake,' she says.

Hunter blushes. If his mum had been on the verandah a few minutes earlier she would have seen him trundling along with his dad's clothes.

The same four men in cycling outfits who were there the other day are sitting at an outdoor table. The man with the yellow bandana is fiddling with his helmet strap. The waitress brings him a slice of lemon meringue pie with a huge mound of cream on top.

'Where have you been, Hunter?' his mum asks, as they sit at a table near an open window. She motions for the waiter to bring a coffee and a thickshake. He knows their usual order.

Hunter looks at the table of cyclists. Bandana-man has a dollop of cream on his knuckles. He wipes it on his jersey and keeps eating.

'Hunter?'

'I was just skating,' Hunter says.

'I could see that, dear,' she says. 'Did you go to the skate park?'

He nods.

The waiter brings his mum's coffee and slides the thickshake across the table to Hunter.

The table of cyclists laugh. One of the cyclists in a red jersey stands and pretends to be riding a bike

146

slowly up a mountain. He sways from side to side, grimacing, before collapsing back into his chair. The men laugh again.

'I finished work thirty minutes early. I couldn't resist a little treat for you,' Mrs Riley says.

Hunter sighs.

'What is it, dear?' His mum reaches across and touches his shoulder.

'I wasn't at the skate park,' Hunter says, taking a deep breath. 'I was ... I took Dad's clothes to the Salvos.'

There, he said it. He reaches for the thickshake, but doesn't take a sip. He hopes his mum doesn't cry. Not in the cafe. Not with all those men around.

'All the boxes?' his mum says.

Hunter nods. 'On my skateboard.'

His mum laughs. She gets up and wraps both arms around Hunter in a big hug. Hunter feels his face pressed into her chest. She strokes his hair.

'Oh, you beautiful boy!' she says.

Hunter squirms free. He notices the table of cyclists looking at him, except Bandana-man. He's scooping up the last of the cream.

'I've been wanting to get rid of them for ages,' Mrs Riley says. 'But I was worried about ...' She shakes her head. 'I'm such a fool.'

She signals to the waiter and sits back down. The man comes from behind the counter.

Hunter looks at his mum. Her eyes are sparkling and her face is flushed. She's smiling. She leans back in the chair and exhales, as if a great weight has been lifted from her shoulders.

The waiter asks if there's a problem.

'Not at all,' Hunter's mum says. She looks at Hunter.

'Let's have a cake, dear.'

Hunter looks at the cyclists.

'Lemon meringue pie, Mum?'

She laughs.

'With double cream. And two forks,' she says.

26

jesse

A few days later on a Wednesday morning, all of Class 6S are standing under an awning, watching the rain fall. I look up at the skyscraper towering above us. The Japanese Embassy is on the sixteenth floor. Office workers hurry past, their heads bowed against the rain. I zip up my black jacket. I was tempted to wear my hoodie but I didn't want to scare the pedestrians. Everyone in my class holds a stack of leaflets, waiting.

Sarah nods. 'Now remember, don't force anyone to take one. Just offer it with a smile.'

I step forward, nervously offering a leaflet to a man wearing a suit and carrying an umbrella. He looks at me and brushes past. A man in shorts and a fluoro vest rushes toward me. He's carrying a parcel under one arm. I smile.

'Not today, mate,' he says.

Next, a bicycle courier jumps the gutter and rides past. Rain drips from his helmet. He shakes his head as I step forward. I look across at Kate. She's standing in the middle of the footpath, handing out leaflets to everyone as they walk past. Most people ignore her, but she walks alongside them until they relent and take the paper from her hands. She keeps repeating, 'Save the whales,' or, 'You can change the world'.

When she runs out of leaflets, she rushes back to Sarah and grabs another bundle. The rest of the class are standing in twos and threes, taking turns to offer the leaflet. No-one seems particularly enthusiastic. Skye is yawning under the awning.

There's no sign of newspaper reporters or television cameras to record our protest.

A lady with a shopping trolley approaches me. I smile at her. 'Would you like a leaflet?' I ask. 'It's about the whales.'

She takes the leaflet and studies it.

'Whales?' she says.

'Yes, the Japanese are,' I don't really want to say the word killing to this nice old lady, 'hurting them.'

'Oh, that's not fair,' she says, tucking the leaflet into the top of her shopping trolley. 'I'll talk to Gerald about that.'

'Who's Gerald?' I ask.

The old lady stops walking and smiles. 'You know my Gerald, do you?' She reaches out a hand and touches my wrist. 'Lovely man, my Gerald.'

'Yes,' I stammer, not sure what else to say.

'SAVE THE WHALES,' yells Hunter. The old lady jumps and lifts her hand to her mouth.

'Don't worry, he's harmless,' I say.

'My goodness. Where was I?' she mutters.

'Gerald,' I prompt.

'Yes, Gerald's father fought the Japanese in the war, you see. He'll stop them. Of course, I haven't seen much of him lately,' she says, quietly. 'Not since he ...' She looks skyward.

'Heaven,' I say.

She laughs and looks at me strangely. 'No, silly. He's managing director, with a new office on the twenty-second floor. Lovely view.'

She pats my hand. 'Well, I best be going. Good luck with the ...'

'Whales.'

'And the Japanese,' she adds.

The rain falls steadily. Sarah and the class huddle together under the awning. Kate and I are the only ones still in the rain. I've only got a few leaflets left. Kate is walking around gathering more leaflets from the rest of the class and frantically handing them out. I give my last leaflet to a tourist, who looks at it and hands it back, saying, 'No Ingleesh'.

I stuff the leaflet into my pocket and walk toward Sarah.

'Well done, Jesse,' Sarah says, 'but I'm afraid we have another stack of leaflets in my bag.'

'I'm hungry,' says Skye.

Sarah sighs.

Kate walks back to the group. She looks at Sarah, hopefully. 'Have we heard from the embassy? Are they going to send somebody down to meet us?'

Sarah checks her mobile phone and shakes her head.

'I'm hungry,' repeats Skye and a few others join in. Hunter starts walking toward McDonald's.

'Hunter, you know that's against school policy.'

'Food is against school policy,' Hunter says.

'Multinational corporations,' says Sarah. 'We'll find a small kiosk, or maybe we can go to the food court.'

'Not Japanese,' says Kate. 'I'm starting a boycott.' She crosses her arms. 'I'm not buying anything made in Japan.'

'What sort of car does your mum drive?' Hunter asks.

Kate ignores him and walks toward the food court. The rest of us follow her. Sarah says, 'Hunter, could you try to be more supportive, please?'

'Sure, Sarah.'

We all wait for the punchline, but Hunter just smiles and walks on ahead.

In the food court, Sarah orders huge plates of Chinese dumplings.

'Dumplings are for fatties,' Skye moans.

'Yeah, dumplings for dumplings,' adds Anastasia.

Sarah looks reproachfully at both of them. 'We've made a communal decision, girls.'

'What does that mean?' asks Anastasia.

'Sarah says dumplings, we eat dumplings,' interrupts Hunter.

'That's not true, Hunter. I asked everyone what they wanted,' says Sarah.

'Yeah, and we all said no to everything,' answered Hunter.

'So that's why I chose dumplings,' says Sarah.

'I like dumplings,' I say.

'Who asked you, Jesse?' says Skye.

I go back to eating dumplings. While they're arguing, there's more food for the rest of us.

'Okay, you three can choose whatever you want from the food court but don't wander out of my sight.'

Hunter salutes. Anastasia and Skye giggle and walk straight to Pizza Hut. Hunter wanders around the food court until he reaches the sushi stand. He studies the menu before ordering. The girl he orders from retreats into the kitchen and a man in a white shirt and tie comes out to talk to Hunter. During the conversation, they bow a number of times at each other, before Hunter carries his food back to our table.

As soon as he sits down, Kate says, 'How can you eat sushi?'

'Simple, I open my mouth and chew.'

Everyone at the table laughs.

'Don't you feel bad,' says Kate, 'supporting whale killers?'

'It's,' Hunter holds up the sushi, 'chicken, not whale.' He makes a clucking sound from the back of his throat. 'And,' he waits until everyone is listening, 'Sarah, you said you had more leaflets?'

Sarah nods, uncertainly.

Hunter smiles. 'The sushi owner has asked me if he could display the leaflets on his counter.' Hunter can barely contain his excitement. 'His staff will hand them out to the customers.' He sits back in his chair, satisfied.

'Wow,' says Kate. 'That's genius!' She smiles at Hunter. 'I take it all back, Hunter.'

'Very impressive,' adds Sarah.

Kate says, 'We could print more leaflets and leave them at every sushi stand in the city.'

Everyone moans, except me and Hunter.

He looks at Sarah. 'Sarah, can I have every morning off school next week to deliver the leaflets? To save the whales?'

'Good try, Hunter,' says Sarah. 'I don't think Larry will agree to you wandering the streets when you should be in class.'

154

'It's for a good cause,' I offer. Keep Hunter out of class for as long as possible, I think.

'Thanks, comrade,' says Hunter.

'The answer is no, Hunter,' says Sarah. 'But I'm happy for you to draft a letter to each of the sushi shops in town and we'll send them the leaflets.'

'I could do it, Sarah,' interrupts Kate.

Hunter shrugs. 'It's all yours, Protest Girl.'

'Name calling, Hunter,' says Sarah.

'Thanks, Sarah,' answers Hunter.

Sarah sighs again.

27
HUNTER

Hunter walks to his bedroom window, pulls the curtain open and looks out to the street below. A dog wanders down the footpath, sniffing in the grass. It cocks its back leg against a fence and piddles. Hunter opens the window and whistles. The dog pricks its ears and lifts its leg, as if waiting for a signal. Hunter whistles again. The dog runs off down the street. He watches until the dog is out of sight.

He thinks of the excursion today. How everyone stood around under the awning, watching the rain fall, while Jesse and Kate handed out leaflets. He knew there had to be a better way. He'd stuffed the leaflets into his jacket pocket. No way was he handing them out to people who'd throw them away once they walked around the corner.

When he saw the sushi shop at lunch, he couldn't resist. The girl behind the counter had asked for his order. Hunter bought two chicken teriyaki rolls, before asking, 'Can I speak to the manager?' No please, no whining voice, just a simple request. When the manager arrived, Hunter was glad he was Japanese. Hunter bowed. The manager bowed in response.

'My father is managing director of Dalton Enterprises,' said Hunter. 'They own the Dalton building, just around the corner.' Hunter remembered the name of the building easily, they'd all been staring at it for an hour in the rain. 'They have one hundred and ten workers,' Hunter paused, letting the number hang, 'and my father is planning a surprise party for the anniversary of the company.' Hunter cast his eyes along the array of sushi behind glass at the front counter. The manager noticed and seemed to half-bow once again, before reaching into his pocket for a business card and offering it to Hunter. Hunter smiled and pretended to read the card. 'Will you be able to supply that much food?' Hunter asked.

The manager beamed. 'Certainly, just ask your father to call me, anytime.'

Hunter tapped the card on the counter. 'Expect a call this week, sir.' He turned, then hesitated. 'One more question, sir?' The manager leaned forward.

'Where do you, I mean where does your company, stand on the issue of whales?'

The manager looked confused. 'Whales?' He looked at his array of food, as if he was caught serving something illegal. 'Whales?' he repeated.

'Dalton Enterprises is a ...' Hunter searched for the right word. What would Kate say? 'An environmentally committed company. They could not buy off anybody who supported the killing of—'

'We understand. No whales.' The manager brightened. 'Chicken.'

Hunter removed the leaflets from his jacket and offered them to the manager. 'Perhaps you'd put these leaflets on the counter? It's a Dalton ...' He couldn't think of the word.

The manager took the leaflets and studied them. He frowned.

'Of course, if you don't wish to support ...' Hunter held out his hand as if to take them back.

The manager gripped the leaflets. 'No. It's okay,' he replied, placing the stack of leaflets beside the cash register. 'We support,' he glanced at the leaflets and attempted to smile, 'the whales.'

Hunter nodded. 'I'm off to see my father after lunch. I'll be sure to tell him about this.' He bowed again, careful not to smile until he was facing his schoolfriends.

Hunter turns from the window and sits at his desk. He remembers the looks on Kate and Jesse's faces when he told the class what he'd achieved. For once his 'father' was useful, he thought.

'Hunter?' Mrs Riley stands at the entrance to his bedroom.

'Hi, Mum.' He blushes, even though he knows she can't read his thoughts. No-one can.

'I want to talk to you,' she looks nervously out the window, 'about … something.' She attempts a smile. 'I bought some chocolate eclairs.' She turns and walks downstairs to the kitchen.

Hunter hopes it's nothing to do with his father and New Zealand.

The kettle whistles in the kitchen. His mother leans against the counter, staring at the steam. Hunter walks across the kitchen and removes the kettle from the stove.

'I'm sorry, Mum,' he says, wondering why he's apologising.

He sees the teapot on the table, the lid already off, the tea-leaves black against the white china. He pours the boiling water over the leaves and replaces the lid. Hunter returns the kettle to the stove, waiting for his mum to speak. She still hasn't moved.

They stand in the kitchen for what seems like hours before she sits down at the table and gestures for him to join her.

'I'm sorry, dear,' she begins.

Why are they both apologising?

'I want to talk to you about,' she blushes, 'something I want to try. But I won't do it unless you think it's okay.'

Please don't let it be moving to New Zealand, Hunter thinks. He notices his fists are clenched on the kitchen table, waiting, expecting the worst.

Mrs Riley presses her hands hard against her temples as if she's trying to stop herself from thinking too much. Hunter reaches across to touch his mother's shoulder. 'It's okay, Mum,' he says, nervously. 'Whatever you do is okay.' Except New Zealand, he thinks.

To stop his mind from racing, Hunter grips the teapot and pours the brew. When the cup's full, he gently pushes it across the table toward his Mum. He takes the chocolate eclairs from the brown paper bag and places them on a plate.

'I want to look for a friend,' his mother whispers, 'on the internet.' She glances at her son.

'A friend?' Hunter repeats. 'An old schoolfriend?' he asks.

His mother laughs. 'No. A man friend,' she says. She takes a sip of tea, the steam rising from the cup. 'To go out for lunch sometimes. Maybe a picnic. Or an afternoon at the beach. To help me forget your ...' She looks hopefully at Hunter.

He knows what she means. Anyone but Dad. He imagines his mum placing an advertisement on dating sites. *Friendly, caring woman looking for anyone. Anyone but my ex-husband.* He wishes he could do the same. *Boy seeking Dad, for friendship and afternoon footy games. Must not own sports cars and frisbees.*

'I won't go out at night.' His mother reaches for his hand. 'Only lunch. Just for the company.'

Hunter nods, unable to speak. What if he doesn't like her new friend? What if the man asks Mum to marry him? Who wouldn't want to be with his mum. What if the new man has children of his own? And they have to move in together? He's thrown out his father's clothes only to replace them with a sonky half-brother who whines and cries and wants Hunter to watch dorky TV shows and help him with science experiments. What if the man calls him Hunts? Hunter shivers.

His mother clanks the cup back on the saucer. 'Let's forget I said anything.' She picks up a chocolate eclair, but doesn't take a bite. She puts it back into the paper bag and carries it to the bench. She looks out the window and sighs.

Hunter looks at the single eclair, lonely on the plate. He takes a deep breath. 'It's okay, Mum. I understand.' Maybe it's like getting a new teacher every year at school. It takes a while to get used to them, but eventually everyone learns to cope. The teacher does what they do and Hunter spends lots of time asking if he can go to Walter.

Mrs Riley turns and walks toward Hunter. She reaches for him and he presses his cheek against her stomach, closing his eyes. Her arms wrap around his shoulders. She strokes his hair and laughs. 'Why would I need anyone else but you, Hunter?'

Hunter keeps his eyes closed and repeats, 'It's okay, Mum. You can have ...' He forces the words out, 'Just not like Dad.' He turns his face toward her dress and starts to cry.

28

jesse

Dinner is a bowl of plain rice, two yams each and a glass of rainwater, direct from our tank. Mum carries a jug of gravy to the table and places it beside the salt and pepper shakers. 'I thought we might need something to ...' She glances at Dad.

'Make it edible?' says Beth.

'Enhance the flavour,' answers Mum.

Dad coughs and looks from Mum to me. 'Jesse,' he reaches for a glass of water and takes a sip, 'we've decided that this month is the last. We don't think—'

'We can't keep donating to your friend, Jesse,' Mum interrupts.

'Great, no more of this food!' says Beth.

'Beth,' says Mum, 'could you try to be a little more sensitive, please.'

'It's okay,' I say.

'Really, Jesse?'

I nod. Poor Kelifa. Now he's stuck with four sisters, no mother and no money. I don't really feel hungry any longer. Dad reaches across the table and touches my arm. 'We're sorry, son, but with your mum having her hours cut back and excursion fees and—'

Mum sighs. 'If I get more work, we'll think about it again, okay Jesse?'

'Sure,' I say. 'Kate and I were talking about taking up a collection at school, but we've been too busy with the whales.'

We all concentrate on eating our yams and rice. Beth tips half the jug of gravy on her rice and spoons it through. 'Mmm, salt and starch, what more could a young girl need,' she winks at me, 'other than a bucket to vo—'

'Beth!'

'Sorry, Mum, it's delicious.'

I finish my yams and rice and ask to be excused.

'Of course, Jesse. Beth's happy to stack the dishwasher tonight.' Mum looks meaningfully at Beth.

'How could I say no, after such a meal,' answers Beth.

In my bedroom, I sit on the floor looking up at Trevor. He appears to be offering sympathy, his arms spread wide.

'Kelifa needs food, not ...' I sigh. Beth's right. I should stop talking to myself. It's my fault. I should never have stolen Dad's credit card, or made my parents feel guilty, forcing them to spend more than they can afford. Some things are too big for a boy to solve. Like feeding the starving poor or stopping the Japanese killing all those whales. I close my eyes. The vision of a harpoon firing and exploding into the shiny skin of a minke whale makes me shiver. I feel like crying.

I wonder what Kelifa does when he feels things are too big for him. Does he talk to his dad? Or his sisters? He can't sit alone in his room, because he doesn't have a room. Maybe he has a favourite tree he sits in.

I stand and step carefully onto my bed, reaching up to Trevor.

'Sorry,' I say, averting my eyes from his gaze. With shaking hands I remove the Blu Tack from the wall, careful not to tear the poster. Maybe I can give him to the Salvos. They could put him on the wall of their shop on Beaumont Terrace. I flop down on my bed and roll the poster before putting it into the top drawer of my desk. I shape the Blu Tack into a huge ball and throw it against the wardrobe door, time and time again. Not once does it stick. I turn off the light, climb into bed and pull the sheets up high. A stream of streetlight shines on the wall where Trevor once hung.

I whisper to myself, 'Dear Kelifa, I hope you and your sisters don't go hungry. I hope another family, somewhere in the world, has enough money to spare. Maybe your dad will grow a huge crop of yams. I could send you the recipe for gravy.'

'Dear whales, I hope the Japanese stopping hurting you. I hope all the other countries tell them it isn't fair to hunt you in Antarctica.'

I sigh.

I close my eyes.

And fall asleep.

29
jesse

'We should have stormed the embassy,' says a voice from behind me.

I'm standing at the end of the track, looking at the 'Thought for the Day'. It reads:

Help others, before yourself.

Hunter steps forward and reads the sign. He spits beside his feet. 'We should have smashed a few windows,' he says. 'It would have made the news and everyone would know about what they do to whales.'

'Maybe if they read our leaflet, they'll understand,' I suggest.

'Ha!'

I don't know how to answer that, so I shuffle my feet and try not to think of the leaflets piling up in the rubbish bin outside the embassy. Hunter and I stand together, not speaking. A storm bird starts calling from the swamp gum beside Edith. A dark cloud lurks over the trees. It's going to rain before the bell goes for the start of class.

'Ha!' says Hunter again, before walking away.

The first drop lands at my feet, kicking up the dirt. I start walking toward Doris. The rain begins pelting down. Hunter stops walking and looks up at the clouds. I rush past him and reach the verandah of Doris where a few parents are sheltering.

Hunter stands in the courtyard, rain splashing on his forehead. His eyes are closed, his mouth open, drinking the rainwater. I look at the two parents beside me, hoping they'll call out to Hunter. One mother buttons up her jacket, while the other explains that her son, Willow, shouldn't be forced to partner just any child during sports afternoon.

Hunter drops his bag at his feet and shakes the rainwater from his stubbly hair. Suddenly a huge clap of thunder bursts from the sky and both parents beside me jump.

'What's that boy doing?' one mother asks.

'Someone should tell him to move,' the other replies.

Then they go back to talking about Willow.

I unstrap the bag from my back and toss it next to the front door of Doris.

'Hunter,' I call.

He doesn't answer, just leans his head back further to catch more raindrops. Lots of students are arriving at school now, their parents escorting them past Hunter. Everyone is carrying an umbrella. A man holding the hand of his young daughter stops beside Hunter and says, 'You better get out of the rain, buddy'. Hunter ignores him and the daughter leads her father to Edith.

The clouds rumble and in the distance, lightning graffitis the sky. Water rushes down the track. The noise on the tin roof of Doris makes it hard for me to hear what the parents are saying anymore. Probably still talking about Willow.

I can't stand it any longer. I rush out into the storm yelling, 'Hunter!'

He ignores me, his eyes still closed, his face pointing upward. Rainwater trickles down my back, making me shiver. I reach out a hand and grab Hunter's arm. 'Come on, Hunter,' I say. He opens his eyes as if awakening from a dream.

'The storm!' I shout.

'Yeah,' he says, 'it's great, isn't it?' He looks at my hand locked around his arm. 'Are you scared?' he says.

The thunder rumbles again, getting closer.

'It's just water,' adds Hunter.

The thunder claps overhead in a mighty burst. I dig my fingers into Hunter's arm.

'Hey!' he cries out.

I let go of his arm.

'It's only thunder,' he says.

My hair and clothes are soaked. I can feel my teeth shaking with the cold.

Hunter says, 'Were you born scared?'

'Were you born stupid,' I answer, without thinking.

I'm expecting Hunter to jump on me and start punching, but all he does is smile.

'Ha! Good answer, Bleakboy.' He looks up to the sky. 'It's like having a shower outdoors!'

I can feel the water sloshing into my Volleys. It'll be hours before I'm dry. Sarah will call Mum and ask her to bring a change of clothes to school. Mum will miss her yoga class.

'You two boys, out of the rain now!' yells Larry, standing under Doris's verandah.

I turn back to Doris. Hunter doesn't move.

'What's with you, Hunter?' I ask.

'Ha!' he says.

'That's not an answer,' I shout. 'You're just—' I bite my tongue, afraid of saying something I'll regret.

'What, Rainman?'

'You're just trying to act tough because you're weak!' I swallow hard. The rain drips into my eyes and I rub it away.

'What did you say?' Hunter's voice is quiet.

If I repeat it, he'll jump on me.

The music sounds for the start of class. It's an old disco song, a woman singing, 'I can't stand the rain', over and over. I can't help but laugh.

Hunter opens his mouth to catch the raindrops again. He looks up once more to the sky and starts moving in time with the music: a rain dance!

Larry steps into Doris and grabs an umbrella, opens it under the verandah and starts walking toward us. Hunter sees him, picks up his bag and starts walking away toward Arnold. I scurry to the shelter of Doris. Larry follows Hunter until they're both out of the downpour. I'm too far away to hear what Larry is saying but Hunter appears to be listening. The rainwater drips from my clothes and makes a puddle at my feet. I'm shivering, but not from the cold. I've never said anything like that to another person. I'm not sure if I should apologise. Or should I be proud of myself for fighting back?

One of the mothers looks at me and says, 'You should get a towel and dry your hair'.

30

Jesse

I finish my vegemite sandwich, toss the wrapping paper into the bin and trudge to Arnold. Sarah is waiting in our room, sitting at her desk and writing in a notebook. I knock. She beckons me inside.

I sit on my chair and sigh.

Sarah attempts a smile. 'Two detentions in a term. Not a good start, Jesse.'

Detention. For getting soaked to the skin trying to save my worst enemy. According to Larry it's 'for putting yourself in danger'. It's Larry who's putting me in danger, leaving me in detention with Hunter!

As if on cue, Hunter walks into the room without knocking. He shuffles to his chair near the window, flops down and stares outside toward freedom.

Sarah checks her watch. 'Hunter, good of you to join us.'

Hunter doesn't answer.

Sarah closes her notebook and stands. 'I trust I can leave you two together while I go to Doris.'

I raise my hand.

'Yes, Jesse?'

'May I get a book?'

Sarah points to the bookcase along the side wall. She looks meaningfully at Hunter. 'Please don't make me have to return early.' She closes the door and walks along the verandah.

I glance toward Hunter. He's still staring out the window. I get up from my chair and walk to the bookcase. I don't really want to read, but if I have my head buried in a book maybe Hunter will ignore me. As if a book can save me. Standing close to the bookshelf, I close my eyes and reach out. Wherever my hand lands, I'll read that book. I open my eyes. A novel titled *Stormchaser*. Without thinking, I laugh, remembering why Hunter and I are on detention. The perfect book!

'What's so funny, Badboy?' says Hunter.

'Nothing,' I say. I should have remembered where I was. I take the book back to my chair and open it, pretending to read. Hunter gets up and walks toward the front of the room. I slink down further in my chair. He casually picks up a marker and stands in front of the whiteboard. He starts writing, in a clear large text:

STEALING
TRIPPING KENDRICK NORRIS
THREATENING TO PUNCH HARRY
WILSON-HOLMES

Hunter steps back from the whiteboard, considering what he's written.

'What … What are you doing?' I ask.

'What does it look like?' Hunter turns to face me, looking at the book in my hands. 'It's better than reading,' he says.

'I mean, what are you writing?'

'Words,' he says.

We both smile. I can't help myself. 'Very funny,' I decide to risk it, 'Jokeboy!'

Hunter laughs, pointing his finger at me, as if he were firing a gun. I duck, dropping my book on the floor. Hunter walks toward me and leans down to pick up the book. He carries it back to the shelf. He adopts the voice of a teacher, 'Now Jesse, the book will remain here until you learn how to treat school property properly!'

He repeats, 'Property properly!'

Hunter walks back to the whiteboard and points at the word, STEALING.

'One week's detention for stealing Harley Rae's iPod. No-one believed I found it over by the wattle trees where stupid Harley dropped it.'

Hunter points at the next sentence. 'Kendrick just fell over my foot. It's not my fault he's clumsy.'

He writes the word, SMOKING on the board. 'Oh yeah, it wasn't me that got caught for that was it Mr Jones?' He draws a line through the word.

He points to the last sentence. 'Threatening.' He scoffs. 'Not actually hitting anyone, just threatening. Pretending. Ha! Detention for doing nothing. I'd have been better off actually hitting hyphen-Harry.' Hunter flops down in Sarah's chair and puts his feet up on her desk. I look toward the door, expecting Sarah to walk in at any moment.

'Come on,' says Hunter. 'Relax.'

I check my watch. We have another twenty minutes of detention.

'Why were you threatening Harry?' I ask.

Hunter shrugs. 'Some people just ask to be annoyed.'

'And some people are just annoying,' I counter.

Hunter looks up. 'You're pretty smart ...' He's trying to think of a new name.

I suggest, 'Brainboy?'

Hunter looks back at the whiteboard, without answering. He gets up and writes, in large letters:

CALLING PEOPLE NAMES

He laughs to himself, then adds two exclamation marks in bold type.

Satisfied, he sits down again at Sarah's desk.

'It's called bullying,' I say.

'Ha!'

'Haboy!' I respond.

'You see,' says Hunter, 'that doesn't hurt me!'

'But … But for some kids, it does,' I say.

Hunter rolls his eyes, as if he's heard it all before. Which he probably has.

'What do your parents say,' my voice is a little shaky, 'when you get in trouble?'

Hunter stares at his shoes on Sarah's table. He doesn't answer.

'If Mum and Dad found out I got detention, they'd—'

'That's your parents, not mine,' says Hunter.

'Sorry,' I say. 'I guess they've got other things—'

'Don't talk about my parents!' Hunter smacks the desk hard with his hand.

I shake my head, too scared to speak.

Hunter pushes back Sarah's chair and stares out the window. I notice his hands are shaking. All of a sudden, he doesn't look so tough, just sad.

We sit in silence.

I lean back on my chair and clumsily put my feet on the desk.

Hunter looks at me and almost smiles.

I whistle, trying to appear more relaxed than I feel. I tilt back my chair until it's balancing on two legs.

'My dad lives in New Zealand,' Hunter says.

I stop whistling.

'Do you visit?' I ask, nervously.

'He hasn't asked me.' Hunter shakes his head. 'He's never coming back.'

I picture waiting in my bedroom every afternoon for Dad to arrive home and give me a hug. How I'd feel if that suddenly stopped. I imagine Mum and Beth and me at dinner, all of us eating in silence, remembering Dad's bad jokes. How quiet it'd be around home, as if all the life was sucked out the front door one morning, never to return.

'Jesse, tell me what's bad?' Hunter asks.

'Pardon?' I don't understand.

Hunter gets out of the chair and picks up Sarah's ruler. He points it toward the whiteboard and calls out, in a teacher's voice, 'Stealing, bad'. He taps the whiteboard with the ruler. 'Tripping people, very bad.' He waves the ruler over the next word. 'Smoking! Very, very bad.' He points down the list. 'Calling people names!' He turns to look at me. 'A week's detention and a note home to your parents, Hunter Riley.'

He taps the ruler against his leg. 'You are a misguided boy, Hunter. You are disruptive in class and rude and—'

Suddenly he throws the ruler, with every ounce of his strength, toward the window. It sails through the air, making a weird whirring sound before clattering against the pane and landing on the floor. Hunter is flushed with anger. 'Tell me what's worse.' He points at the board. 'All of these things,' he takes a deep breath and flops down on Sarah's chair, his fists clenched on the desk, 'or a father who runs away.'

We sit in silence for a few moments.

'Maybe my dad should be on detention, not me,' Hunter says, bitterly.

Suddenly, all his actions make sense.

I understand. But, there's no way I can tell him that. So, I do the next best thing.

I say, 'Your dad's a ...' I swear, a rude word I never say. I'm shaking, not sure how Hunter will react.

Hunter looks surprised, even a little shocked.

I blush and say it again.

He stands up and walks to the whiteboard. In big letters, he writes another word:

SWEARING!

Hunter smiles.

'Your dad's a ...' I repeat the rude word.

'My dad's a ...' swears Hunter.

We look at one another and together, start laughing.

178

'Rudeboy!' I say.

'Ha!' Hunter laughs.

Sarah opens the door and walks into the room. She glances at the whiteboard and frowns. 'What's this?'

I answer quickly, 'Sorry, Sarah. I … I was getting Hunter to list the things he's done lately and …'

'And Jesse was telling me how to improve,' adds Hunter.

Sarah looks from Hunter to me and back again, not sure if we're serious. She eventually smiles and walks to the whiteboard, erasing each of the words slowly. Hunter looks back at me and flashes a grin.

When Sarah has finished, she turns and says, 'Wiped clean, Hunter. Let's forget all about the past shall we?'

'No worries, Sarah,' says Hunter, before heading toward the door.

Sarah looks at me. 'Thank you, Jesse.'

31

HUNTER

After school, Hunter walks to Elkhorn Park and sits on the bench seat, waiting for the woman and her personal trainer to arrive. He wonders if Les will pass by on his way home from the shops. He hopes so.

A tiny grasshopper lands on the seat. Hunter cups his hands around the insect. He gently carries it to the nearest shrub, giggling as the grasshopper jumps around his hands, tickling his skin. He places his hands amongst the leaves and opens them slowly. The grass-hopper hops to the nearest branch. Hunter watches it for a few minutes before returning to the bench seat.

This morning before school, Hunter had shut himself in his bedroom and typed 'Dating Hearts' into Google. Thousands of listings came up. He typed, with shaking hands, 'Man forty years'. He added the local area into the advanced search listings. A screen popped up with all the available candidates. If only he could remember the man from the cafe, who thought Mum was someone called Diane. Perhaps they could meet again.

ScubaBen was forty-eight years old, one hundred and eighty-five centimetres tall and his byline read, 'Willing to open jars and assemble IKEA furniture. No babysitting required.' What did that mean? In the photo, his eyebrows were too close together. Hunter clicked forward.

Marty42 looked younger and had wavy red hair. 'Easy-going happy-go-lucky every-day single-guy.' Too many hyphens! Hunter shook his head. This could be harder than he first thought.

Paddy2 was thirty-eight years old, wore a suit and tie and was balding. 'Fun-loving, extrovert, independently wealthy.' Hunter clicked on the profile. 'I love sailing, football and long walks.' Mum likes to walk and I like football, thought Hunter. 'Seeks genuine woman under the age of 30.' Hunter shrugged. Mum looked younger than she was. 'Definitely, no kids!' Hunter sighed and said, 'Goodbye Paddy2.'

He stared out the window. Mrs Betts was watering her roses along the front fence. Occasionally, she'd lean down and pull up a weed. When she did, she'd keep the hose spraying, without looking where it was pointing. While Hunter was watching, she'd sprayed the driveway, just missed the postman and unwittingly soaked Mrs Ainsworth's dog.

Jeff50 smiled at the camera and emphasised that age was not important. 'Friendly, educated traveller along life's highway seeks humanist fun-seeker with kind mien.' Hunter frowned, what's a mien?

Barry48 wanted three things in a relationship. 'Eyes that won't cry, lips that won't lie and love that won't die.' Oh yeah, and, 'NO KIDS!'

Hunter clicked forward and came face-to-computer-profile with Donald45, otherwise known as the man in the cafe. He couldn't believe he'd found him so quickly. It was meant to be, thought Hunter. Donald liked 'movies, food and holidays'. Tick, tick, tick, thought Hunter. He scanned the profile. 'Genuine, optimistic, loyal. Seeks the same.' Hunter copied the web address to an email and sent it to his mum. Donald was just one click away, if Mum wished. She's better than any Diane, thought Hunter. Donald smiled from his profile, waiting patiently.

Hunter sees the exercise woman walking along the path beside the creek with her personal trainer. The woman is wearing a dress and high-heeled shoes. The trainer is wearing an open-necked shirt and jeans. They are holding hands and walking very slowly. Neither of them is sweating. The woman says something to the personal trainer and he laughs. He leans across and kisses her on the cheek.

'Young love,' says a voice behind Hunter. Les is sitting on his scooter, a bag of groceries in the basket.

'Okay for some,' says Hunter.

Les reaches into his pocket and takes out a stick of chewing gum, unwraps it and pops it into his mouth. He offers the packet to Hunter. Hunter shakes his head.

'I chew on ten of these a day now, instead of,' he sighs, 'instead of the quiet enjoyment of my pipe.' He scrunches the wrapping paper up in his hand and tosses it into his basket, alongside the groceries.

Hunter smiles, despite himself.

Les moves the scooter closer to the bench seat. They both watch the woman and the trainer walk by, holding hands, peering off into the lover's distance.

'You're quiet today, son,' says Les.

Hunter is surprised by Les's words. He wished his dad had called him son instead of Hunts. He doesn't want to think of his father now. He looks at the old man's hands, brown and aged with sunspots. He thinks about Jesse and swearing in class. Jesse trying to drag him from the thunderstorm, trying to be his friend.

'Do you miss your wife, Les?' he asks.

'Only when I'm awake,' Les says, his hands reaching into his pocket in reflex, searching for the pipe that isn't there anymore. The old man clears his throat. 'Fifty-two years we were together.' He sighs.

'Do you visit ... Do you go to where she's ...' Hunter doesn't want to say the word.

'We made a deal, before she passed,' says Les. 'She didn't want to be underground.' Les takes the chewing gum from his mouth and rolls it in a tight ball, putting it into the plastic grocery bag. He licks his lips as if trying to remove the taste of the gum. 'We decided on cremation,' he says. 'I kept her ashes with me, in an urn on the kitchen bench for months. We'd talk every night.' Les looks at Hunter and smiles. 'I did most of the talking, you understand. We'd agreed beforehand on where I was to place her ashes, but I needed time. Finally, I scattered them at the foot of the pear tree in our backyard. Our daughter is under strict instructions to place mine there when I cark it. So we'll be together.' The old man leans back on his scooter, as though the words he's spoken have exhausted him. He closes his eyes to the sun.

Hunter studies the old man's face: the lines and wrinkles, the grey stubble, the upturned mouth as though he's spent a lifetime smiling.

'My daughter says I should get married again,' Les scoffs. 'She means well, of course. But my wife was ... It's better to keep her memory close than to try to replace it.'

The woman and the trainer walk toward Hunter and the old man. In the hands of the trainer is an

184

iPhone. He holds it out. 'Would you mind taking a photo of us?' he says to Les.

Les laughs and takes the phone, handing it on to Hunter. 'My boy here, he'll do a better job.'

Hunter takes the phone and stands. He looks at the screen and sees the couple, each with an arm around the waist of the other, smiling. He pushes the button.

When he hands the phone back to the trainer, the woman eagerly looks at the screen to see the result. She smiles at Hunter and says, 'Thank you.' They walk off, holding hands.

32
HUNTER

In the early evening, Hunter stands outside the house, looking over the flowering hedge to the screen door. Hunter looks down the street from where he's come. He didn't think he'd catch Les on his scooter after he left the park, but Hunter ran as fast as he could and spied the old man just as he turned into Rochedale Street. He hears Les inside the house talking to someone. Hunter turns to leave, then remembers Les has a dog. He walks nervously to the front gate and pushes it open. It squeaks, loudly.

A voice comes from behind the screen door. 'Looks like we have a visitor, Deefer.'

Hunter steps forward and closes the gate behind him. Too late to run away now. Les opens the door.

'My boy,' he says. 'Did I leave something behind in the park?'

Hunter is not sure why he's here.

Les seems to understand Hunter's nervousness. He says, 'I tell you what, Hunter. Go round the back and you'll see a garden seat under the pear tree. I'll be right out. You can meet Deefer, after he's had a feed. That way he won't mistake you for dinner.' The old man winks.

The screen door slams and Hunter hears the old man shuffling down the hallway. Hunter walks along the overgrown garden path beside the house, careful not to hit his head on the electricity box jutting out from the side wall.

The backyard is neatly mown, with raised corrugated-iron garden beds where lettuce, spinach and tomatoes grow in the rich dark soil. A net is haphazardly strung over a cherry tree in the corner. Hunter looks toward the back door. He sees a pair of green wellington boots covered in dirt on the top step. He walks over to the cherry tree and reaches under the net to pick a ripe berry. He takes a tentative bite. It's sweet and juicy.

In the centre of the garden is a shady tree, with a bench seat underneath. Around the base of the tree is a circular garden of bright orange flowers. Hunter walks to the seat, but doesn't sit down. He leans close to the tree and sees the little green fruit starting to grow on every branch. In a month, the tree will be loaded with pears. He wonders if the birds will eat them, or if Les has a bigger net for this large tree. Against the side fence is a garden shed, with a single wooden chair near the door. Hunter walks over to the chair and carries it back to the pear tree. He sits on it.

The rear door slams. Les holds a tray with a plate of Anzac biscuits and two glasses of frothy drink that looks like beer. 'Can you carry this, Hunter?' Les asks. Hunter jumps up and takes the tray. The old man reaches for his walking stick beside the door. A shaggy, droopy-eared dog, coloured dirty brown with black spots, walks beside them.

Les flops down on the bench seat and Hunter sits on the wooden chair. Les takes the tray from Hunter and puts it on the seat. The dog sniffs Hunter's fingers and licks his hand.

'Deefer and I never have visitors, Hunter,' says Les. 'So, I opened the good stuff.'

Hunter eyes the glass of beer.

'Don't worry, lad, it's ginger beer. Brewed it myself. Guaranteed no alcohol, but still lots of kick.' Les takes a glass and has a long swig. Hunter does the same. When he swallows, he hiccups. Les laughs.

'I warned you!'

Deefer lies down at Les's feet and closes his eyes.

Hunter takes another sip, slowly this time. He looks again at the small fruit on the pear tree.

Les notices and reaches behind the seat to touch the tree trunk. 'When the fruit ripens this year, I'm going to make pear cider.' He looks at Hunter. 'Alcoholic and much tastier than beer!' A siren sounds in the distance and Deefer whines. Les reaches down to rub his neck. The dog settles immediately.

Hunter remembers the joy he felt riding Les's mobility scooter. How Les seemed to know that he would. He recalled the smile on Les's face when he sped back to the seat in the park. He knows he can trust the old man.

'I don't see my dad anymore,' Hunter says. He looks down at his shoes before continuing, 'He ran away'. Hunter thought it was only children who were supposed to run away. And, even then, only for a few hours. Not forever.

Hunter feels his knees shaking. He reaches for the glass to calm himself and takes a quick sip. He dare not look at Les, even though he feels the old man is watching him, waiting.

'I hate him,' Hunter says. 'For leaving. And for hurting Mum.'

A fly buzzes above Hunter's glass of ginger beer. The old man sighs, reaches for the plate of biscuits and offers them to Hunter. He takes one and looks at the old man in thanks. They each eat a biscuit, slowly.

After what seems like ages, Les shifts in his seat and says simply, 'We miss what we don't have, without being thankful for what we've got'.

Hunter imagines his mum applying lipstick and make-up in front of the bathroom mirror, wearing a new dress, with stockings and shiny shoes, waiting for her lunch date to arrive. How excited she'll be. He smiles to himself. Maybe making Mum happy is the best way to be happy himself. He'd never thought of that before. Such an easy solution.

Hunter reaches for the glass of ginger beer and takes another sip. He pictures his mum again, walking around the house in her new dress, expecting a knock on the door. The man from the cafe with the nervous smile, standing on the verandah.

Les speaks slowly, 'We come out here every after-noon, Deefer and me, to sit.' He reaches behind the seat and picks a blooming orange flower, breaking it at the stalk and holding it to his nose. 'This is where I put Dorothy's ashes.' Les smiles. 'I pick these flowers each time they bloom and put them in a vase beside her picture in the lounge room.' Les twirls the flower in his hands. 'Dorothy wouldn't like me sitting around and grumbling. Or being too sad. It would be an insult to her spirit.' Les sighs. 'We have to move on, son. No matter what.'

Hunter looks up. He sees the tears welling in the old man's eyes and understands Les is not only talking about himself.

The old man shuffles up from the seat and says, 'What say I fetch you a bottle of ginger beer to take home. You could share it with your mum.' Deefer jumps up and runs ahead of the old man.

Hunter remains in the chair, looking at the flowers in the garden bed. The colours seem brighter and deeper in the evening light.

33

jesse

I look out the window. It's a bright sunny morning. I lean close to the pane and breathe heavily, frosting the glass. With my finger, I draw an outline of the biggest animal in Antarctica: the blue whale. I step back to admire my artwork. Perfect. Not a Japanese whale-boat in sight.

'What do you think, Kelifa?' I say, looking at the picture of my African friend Blu Tacked to my wall. A beam of sunshine lights the wall above his head. Kelifa seems to be smiling, probably because he's received the email I sent to CARE Australia about the fundraising lunchtime we're having at school today, in his honour.

'Maybe we'll raise enough so your dad can build you a new bedroom,' I say, 'away from your sisters.'

'Mum,' Beth calls, 'Jesse's talking to himself again.'

'Jesse,' Mum's voice calls from the kitchen.

'It's okay,' I yell, 'Kelifa is not a false god, he's an eight-year-old boy.'

Beth comes to my door and smiles. 'Not an imaginary friend?'

I look toward the picture of Kelifa and shake my head. Beth walks into my room and places the new CD of The Scrambles on my dresser. Something is scrawled across the cover.

'Ryan got each of the band members to autograph it, even Feral. He said you could auction it on eBay, or at lunchtime today and give the money to Kelifa,' she says.

'Wow, thanks sis.'

'No worries, anything to avoid eating yams again.'

Mum knocks gently on my open door.

'Beth,' she says.

'Mum,' Beth answers.

Mum glances around the room, looking for Trevor. Kelifa smiles down at her.

'What are you hiding behind your back, Mum?' Beth asks.

Mum smiles. She steps into the room and elaborately presents Beth with a pair of yoga pants.

'I bought these yesterday, Beth.'

Beth accepts the present and holds the pants up to the light.

'They're new, Beth. Not second hand.' Mum turns to go and calls behind her, 'I've kept your old pair.'

Beth stands holding the pants, her mouth open in disbelief.

'You see, sis,' I say, 'the world can change.'

At school, Kate is waiting for me at the 'Thought for the Day' sign. The sign reads:

To give is better than to receive.

Kate's wearing her green ribbon and, just for today, a green 'Save the Whales' t-shirt. As I approach, she lifts her pants to reveal her lucky socks. She smiles. 'Too much green is never enough.'

When we get to class, everyone is sitting down, except Hunter who's sitting on Sarah's desk, his heavy shoes tapping on the wooden panel. Sarah hasn't arrived yet.

'Charityboy and Whalegirl,' Hunter says, as we enter. He winks, just to let me know he's kidding. This time.

'You're early, Hunter,' I say.

'The early bird catches ...'

'The worm,' I suggest.

'The teacher off guard,' he answers.

As if on cue, Sarah walks in. 'Hunter, I believe that's my desk you're sitting on.'

Hunter jumps up and says, 'Sorry, Sarah, but as

we're a community, I thought it was *our* desk'. He casually walks toward his chair and sits down. Sarah sighs and places her handbag on her desk. Our desk.

Skye raises her hand. Sarah pretends not to notice.

'Okay, class. It's D-E-A-R time. And we know what that means.'

'Doze Early And Repeatedly?' Hunter calls.

Everyone giggles, even Sarah.

'Don't Eat At Recess!' I add.

'Dead Elephants And Rhinos!' Hunter answers.

Sarah holds up a book, as if to remind us.

Hunter clicks his fingers. 'Of course. Drop Everything And … Retch!'

I can't help myself. 'Ha!'

Sarah makes an extravagant gesture of opening her book.

'Drop Everything And Read,' Skye calls.

Everyone groans. We all knew that.

After reading, Hunter raises his hand, but before he can ask a question, Sarah says, 'Yes, Hunter, you can go to Walter'. Hunter whistles a bouncy tune as he walks out the door. We can hear it echo along the verandah. When Sarah turns to write on the whiteboard, Kate passes me a note. I unfold it under my desk. It's an invitation to her place tonight, for dinner.

I blush.

*

On the grassy area at lunchtime, a few parents have arranged tables in a large semicircle. On each table are items for sale. All the students wander from table to table, looking for treasure among the cast-off toys and books.

A large sign is strung between the two wattle trees in the corner. It reads, 'All proceeds to charity' with a picture of Kelifa pasted into the top corner. I'm busy tying the cord a little tighter, so Kelifa won't get blown away by the wind, when Kate races up and grabs my hand.

'Hunter is setting up his own stall.' She grins.

'No!' I say. 'I wonder what he's selling.'

'Maybe he's offering a joke booth? One dollar a laugh,' Kate says.

'More likely a "Give me a dollar and I won't hit you" booth. He'd make a fortune with that one,' I say.

She leads me across the grass, still holding my hand. We jostle among the kindy kids surrounding the booths. The first person I notice is not Hunter, but an old man with a walking stick. He's standing behind a table laden with sushi! Hunter is beside him, offering a sushi roll to Larry.

'Three dollars Larry, special deal for teachers,' Hunter says.

I notice the sign above the stall, which reads, 'Sushi $2.50'. Larry sees it too, but happily hands over the gold coins.

Hunter spies me and Kate. He spreads his arms wide, a shopkeeper displaying his fine items. 'Chicken, avocado, beef teriyaki,' he says. 'No whale meat!' Kate and I both reach into our pockets.

Hunter makes a gesture for us to stop. He offers me a chicken roll and Kate an avocado and cucumber roll. 'Free for my friends,' he says.

'Did you buy all this?' I ask.

The old man puts his arm around Hunter's shoulder. 'A nice Japanese man gave us a huge discount.' He reaches across the table to shake our hands. 'My name's Les.' He looks at Hunter. 'The young man here told me all about fundraising for the starving Africans,' Les says. 'He figured as I had lots of spare time, I might as well join him on this stall.'

Les reaches behind him into a large esky and pulls out a bottle of fizzy drink. He pours it into two plastic cups for Kate and me. 'Home-brewed ginger beer, on the house. Or on the stall, I should say.'

He leans forward. 'Funny thing is, the Japanese man seemed to think I was Hunter's father and the head of a company called Dalton Enterprises.'

'Hunter can be very ...' I can't think of the correct word.

'Persuasive?' Les suggests.

'Imaginative,' says Hunter.

Les reaches to shake my hand, again. 'This is a good thing you've organised, young man.'

Hunter sees Sarah on the verandah and cups his hands together, calling out, 'Sushi, Sarah! Special price for teachers.'

Sarah reaches for her handbag.

Hunter looks at me. 'I'm going to ask Sarah if you and me and Kate can help pack up, after lunch,' he says. 'That way, we'll miss maths.'

There's only one word I can say in response.

'Ha!'

Helpful Websites

Jesse, Hunter and Kate recommend these services:

www.care.org.au
CARE Australia is an Australian charity and international humanitarian aid organisation fighting global poverty, with a special focus on empowering women and girls to bring lasting change to their communities.

www.msf.org.au
Médecins Sans Frontières (Doctors Without Borders) is an international, independent, medical humanitarian organisation.

kidshelp.com.au
If you're between five and twenty-five and need someone to talk to Kids Helpline is there 24/7 for

problems big and small. Call 1800 551 800. Our services are free.

www.seashepherd.org.au
Sea Shepherd Australia is a non-profit conservation organisation whose mission is to end the destruction of habitat and slaughter of wildlife in the world's oceans in order to conserve and protect ecosystems and species.

SNEAK PEEK ...

POOKIE ALEERA IS NOT MY BOYFRIEND

STEVEN HERRICK

UQP

RACHEL

My town
is exactly
four hundred and twenty-two kilometres
from the ocean.
I check the distance
driving home from holidays
with Mum and Dad
the day before school begins
and while Bondi Beach
gets frothy waves
of cool, salty water on white sand
my town suffers
waves of dust storms
and locust plagues
and heat that melts the bitumen
and the first thing I do
when we get home
after driving all day
is run down to the dam
in the near paddock
and dive in.
The water is warm and brown.

My toes squelch in the mud
while the windmill clanks.
A pond-skater buzzes the surface
and starlings fantail
across the sky
the day before school begins.

LAURA

My new teacher
wears a flowing summer dress
with red pianos printed
on white linen.
Her hair is crow-black and messy
and she pulls it back
from her face
and ties it with a red ribbon.
She wears black ballet shoes
and casually sits on her desk
before asking us
to tell her something, one thing,
that we like about ourselves.
Selina, Mick, Cameron, Pete and Rachel
immediately
raise their hands
while I slink as low as possible
behind my desk.

SELINA

Ms Arthur said we should
bring in a photo of ourselves,
our favourite,
to paste on the Class 6A wall
and we could draw a design
around the photo
with our name, in bright colours.
And underneath our photo
we could write,
once a week,
what we've done lately
or what made us happy, or sad.
'Just like Facebook,' I said.

On Tuesday we spent all morning
drawing our names in big letters
with swirling colours
of red, yellow, green and blue.
Except Cameron
who wrote his name in *tiny letters*.
His writing was so small
you had to go really close

just to see if it was there at all.
And he'd chosen a thumbnail photo
of when he was a baby
lying in a cot asleep.
Cameron spent the whole morning
admiring his *little* photo and his *teeny* name
surrounded by glaring white cardboard.
Sometimes he stepped back
and looked at the photo from different angles,
like an artist.
Then he'd move close and adjust it,
just slightly.
Finally Ms Arthur couldn't stand it any longer.
She asked Cameron
if he planned to add anything
to his cardboard.
Cameron looked shocked
and said, in his usual loud voice,
'No way, Ms.
I want to have lots of space
to write about everything I think!'

MICK

I'm staring out the window
minding no one's business but my own
because Ms Arthur is teaching maths
and that's not really my go.
What do we have calculators for?
Charlie Deakin from 5C comes in with a note
and Ms Arthur tells me the Principal
'requires my presence in his office'.
So I follow Charlie along the verandah
and he's smirking the whole time
because no one gets called out of class
for good news,
it's always trouble,
but I don't say anything
and I don't act nervous
because I haven't done anything wrong,
not lately anyway.
Well, not that Mr Hume knows
and I trust my classmates not to tell anyway.
Charlie Deakin is still grinning
like he's won a prize,
yeah, first-prize boofhead.

He knocks on the Principal's door
and says to me,
'Hume's madder than a nest of bull ants.'
Charlie Deakin opens the door
and walks away down the hallway
leaving me standing there
with Mr Hume looking at me
and he's not smiling.